Totally Bound Publishing books by Ashe Barker:

Darker
Darkest

Sure Mastery
Unsure
Sure Thing
Surefire

The Hardest Word
A Hard Bargain

What's her Secret?
The Three R's

Seasonal Collections
Paramour: Re-Awakening

The Hardest Word

A HARD BARGAIN

ASHE BARKER

A Hard Bargain
ISBN # 978-1-78184-762-6
©Copyright Ashe Barker 2014
Cover Art by Posh Gosh ©Copyright March 2014
Interior text design by Claire Siemaszkiewicz
Totally Bound Publishing

This is a work of fiction. All characters, places and events are from the author's imagination and should not be confused with fact. Any resemblance to persons, living or dead, events or places is purely coincidental.

All rights reserved. No part of this publication may be reproduced in any material form, whether by printing, photocopying, scanning or otherwise without the written permission of the publisher, Total-E-Bound Publishing.

Applications should be addressed in the first instance, in writing, to Totally Bound Publishing. Unauthorised or restricted acts in relation to this publication may result in civil proceedings and/or criminal prosecution.

The author and illustrator have asserted their respective rights under the Copyright Designs and Patents Acts 1988 (as amended) to be identified as the author of this book and illustrator of the artwork.

Published in 2014 by Totally Bound Publishing, Newland House, The Point, Weaver Road, Lincoln, LN6 3QN, United Kingdom.

No part of this book may be reproduced, scanned, or distributed in any printed or electronic form without permission. Please do not participate in or encourage piracy of copyrighted materials in violation of the authors' rights. Purchase only authorised copies.

Totally Bound Publishing is an imprint of Total-E-Ntwined Limited.

If you purchased this book without a cover you should be aware that this book is stolen property. It was reported as "unsold and destroyed" to the publisher and neither the author nor the publisher has received any payment for this "stripped book".

A HARD BARGAIN

Dedication

For Hannah, my current work in progress, and John.

Prologue

From: Freya Stone
To: Nicholas Hardisty
Date: 27 March 2013
Subject: A Business proposal

Dear Mr Hardisty

Please forgive this less than orthodox approach. I was given your contact details by Angela Delaney, who I believe is a mutual acquaintance to both of us. We probably have a number of mutual acquaintances in fact, as we are both members of the Collared and Tied club. Certainly I've seen you there, in the dungeon.

There's no delicate way to frame my proposition, and I appreciate that in normal circumstances a direct approach from me, to you, would not be acceptable. But my circumstances are a little unusual and I hope you will be able to overlook my departure from accepted practice. In short, Mr Hardisty, I want to commission your services. As a Dominant, my Dom, specifically. I am convinced that you would never normally consider inviting me to scene with you, so I feel I should offer you some payment to compensate you for your time and for sharing your expertise. Would you consider the sum of twenty-five thousand pounds to be a fair price for your services? If not, I am happy to negotiate.

For this amount, or whatever sum we eventually agree on, I would wish to enjoy your attention, exclusively, for a period of I think perhaps one month, though, I am prepared to be flexible on that also. You will know better than I what's involved and how long it might take. During that time, I would like you to work with me, train me in order that I can become accustomed to submission and the BDSM lifestyle. I am interested in exploring the various forms of submission, the usual and most common practices and so on. You will appreciate that whilst I have long been aware of this aspect of my nature, my experience is extremely limited, and to date my progress as a submissive has not always been especially rewarding. I have reached the conclusion that unless I take drastic steps, that situation will not alter.

I mentioned that my circumstances are unusual, and I feel I need to explain those to you more fully in order that you can consider my proposal fairly. Whilst I have normal hearing, I am mute. I cannot speak at all and therefore I cannot use safe words or other vocal clues to communicate with a Dom. I have on a number of occasions encountered difficulties as a result of my particular communication challenges. Not that I have had many offers.

On the other hand, I understand that you have an extensive track record and considerable expertise in training submissives, and I would like to be able to benefit from that specialist knowledge.

If you are positively inclined to consider my proposition, perhaps we could arrange a time to get together to discuss the details. I am happy to meet with you at a time and place of your convenience.

Best regards

Freya Stone (Miss)

From: Nicholas Hardisty
To: Freya Stone
Date: 31 March 2013
Subject: NO!

Dear Miss Stone

You are quite correct. Your approach is both unorthodox and inappropriate. I am in the habit of selecting my own submissives, and have never yet found it necessary to do so on the basis of financial consideration.

I understand your membership of the Collared and Tied club has been revoked so it is unlikely our paths will cross again. May I therefore take this opportunity to wish you every success for the future.

And finally, if I were minded to accept payment for my services as you suggest, I would have done what you require for considerably less than you have offered.

N. Hardisty

From: Freya Stone
To: Nicholas Hardisty
Date: 2 April 2013
Subject: A Business Proposal

Dear Mr Hardisty

There was no need to have my membership revoked. A simple no would have sufficed. As there are no other reputable establishments catering to my – our – preferences closer than Glasgow, I now find myself with nowhere safe to play.

I am therefore considerably worse off than when I first approached you. Perhaps that was your intention, but I feel that a more direct form of retribution would have been more appropriate. You could have simply spared a few moments to spank me, and been done with it.

Needless to say, I deeply regret having approached you, and you will not be bothered by me again.
Yours sincerely
Freya Stone (Miss)
P.S. The level of my financial offer reflected the value I place on the service I am seeking. I have the funds, and how I decide to spend my money is entirely up to me.

From: Angela Delaney
To: Nick Hardisty
Date: 2 April 2013
Subject: Freya

Nick

I can't believe you did that. Freya was only asking you to help her. You had only to say no. You and I both know perfectly well that if you'd chosen not to agree, you could have convinced her to abandon her plans without resorting to such measures.

Freya Stone needs her membership in the club. You know as well as I the dangers facing an unattached and inexperienced submissive, let alone a sub with Freya's communication difficulties. Freya is willing, enthusiastic, courageous and honest. She could, given training, become a perfect submissive. And she deserves a chance, no less than the rest of us. I can't imagine how she'll cope now, without the relative safety and protection offered by a well-run club. No doubt she'll be reduced to skulking around dodgy chat rooms and sleazy online networks. Heaven help her.

You may own the club, but I am the manager here. You are also my big brother, Nick, and you know I have the utmost respect for you. I have no wish to quarrel with you, but you make it extremely difficult at times, not least when you take matters of club membership into your own hands in this way. I am very disappointed in you over this, Nick. Very disappointed indeed. I like Freya Stone and I've tried to help her, train her, but it's not a Domme she wants. She will only really respond to a Master, and I don't doubt that she would have responded beautifully, given time and the opportunity to explore her nature in safety.

And regardless of your singularly ill-chosen remarks in your email to me earlier today, I have no regrets at all about suggesting to Freya that you could meet her needs because quite simply, Nick, you could. Can. You are exactly what she needs. As the general manager of this club, I am aware that you are an experienced trainer, highly regarded among all the submissives you've educated. You have a reputation for being hard but fair, exacting and challenging. You certainly have the skill and creativity, and the patience, to devise ways of overcoming Freya's particular issues and developing her unique qualities. And you're intuitive, tuned in to your submissive's responses, good at reading the signals. Even without words, you would know how she was feeling, you'd be aware of her responses whether she was able to tell you or not, and you could have trained her. I know Freya would have been safe with you and that's why I recommended you. And it's not as though you don't have the time, now that you're not throwing tourists out of those bloody planes of yours every day.

I should have insisted though on making the introduction rather than allowing Freya to approach you herself. I did advise her against offering you money for your services, but she felt certain you would not entertain her otherwise. Again though, you had only to say no.

Despite my advice, she was determined to approach you, she felt it was the polite and most reasonable course to take. How wrong she was, and I'm sure she will by now be bitterly regretting it. If you'd bothered to even talk to her, you'd have found out that Freya's lack of speech has made it near enough impossible for her to discuss and negotiate her needs with any of the Doms who she has experimented with so far. She's had some distressing experiences, and it's to her credit that she still has the fortitude to persevere. Or she did. Until she encountered you.

As well as refusing to help her, you have also had her club membership revoked. That last was unnecessary. I want you to re-consider. Please, for me.

Yours
Ange

From: Nicholas Hardisty
To: Freya Stone
C.c. Angela Delaney
Date: 4 April 2013
Subject: Collared and Tied Club

Dear Miss Stone

Your membership at the Collared and Tied club has been reinstated. My actions were disproportionate, and I apologize for any undue distress caused. Your suggestion made in your email of 2 April 2013 is accepted as the more appropriate course of action and therefore when you next encounter me at the club, please be so good as to make yourself known to me and I will administer it.

There is no need to respond to this email. I would prefer no further communication between us other than that outlined above.

N. Hardisty

Chapter One

"That's him." I sign the words to Summer, my closest and dearest friend, who's managed somehow to bury all her own heartfelt objections to this mad scheme of mine and has come here with me anyway. To provide moral support. Or maybe to try one last time to talk me out of it. And if all else fails, as she puts it, to pick up what's left of me afterwards and make sure I get home.

"Who? Which one?" she whispers the questions back at me.

Two powerful-looking Doms lean casually against the bar in the far corner of the members' lounge here at the Collared and Tied club. They're talking quietly, both their expressions serious, and although this is very much a social club and they're both nursing drinks, I suspect their discussion is more business than pleasure. Still, that doesn't concern me. My business with Nicholas Hardisty will definitely have very little to do with pleasure. He's here. And so am I. It's to be tonight then.

It's been over a month now since that disastrous, ill-fated email exchange with the terrifying Mr Hardisty, and I've been dreading this face to face encounter. Twice a week for the last four and a half weeks, I've been dreading it. Each time I've returned here since that awful day when I picked up that voicemail message from the membership secretary telling me that I was considered 'unsuitable for membership' and that therefore my pass card had been invalidated. The cultured female voice went on to inform me that I would not be admitted to the premises again, I was no longer a 'friend' in the club Facebook group and my log-in details had been removed from the club website. And the remainder of my annual membership fee was non-refundable. The cash was the least of my worries, but I was suddenly cut adrift, an outsider, not welcome. Not that I've ever felt especially welcome, more a fish out of water if I'm honest, but I have always felt safe here and that matters to me. I was gutted by what had happened, completely crushed. It never occurred to me that a simple request, however unwanted or uninvited, would result in such harsh and instant retribution.

Mistress Angela spoke up for me, I know I have her to thank. And he relented, commuted my sentence so to speak.

My foster mum always advised me to be careful what I wished for. Well, I certainly wished to attract the attention of the most respected and desirable Dom in the Collared and Tied club, and I've got my wish. And now, he's going to spank me. It'll be a punishment spanking, so I have no illusions. It's going to hurt. A lot. He didn't actually say, didn't say much at all in fact, but I would think it's likely he'll have it in mind to punish me in front of an audience to discourage any other similarly unruly and misguided submissive from breaking the rules and irritating him. Maybe it'll be in the dungeon, so I get to be publicly humiliated as well as hurt.

Not that I'll get any say in it. And there's no point at all in delaying the inevitable. Indeed, if he suspects I've tried to avoid him or delay matters, he'll dish out even more retribution. So it's really got to be now.

Summer finds this fondness of mine for kinky sex more than a little unsettling, but even so she hasn't tried to talk me out of my regular visits to the club. Well, not much. Until now. Ultimately, she's all for consenting adults is Summer, and she just wants me to be happy. And safe. But she doesn't think this latest business with Nicholas Hardisty is even remotely safe, a view she's shared with me pretty much constantly for the last four and a half weeks. Ever since I confided to her what I'd done, and what the consequences were. And what I intended to do — or more accurately allow this powerful and angry Dom to do — in order to resolve the matter.

"You don't have to do this. It's mad. No one can expect you to just walk up to him and, and…"

"Introduce myself as the submissive who pissed him off right royally and who he now gets to spank by way of retribution." My hands are moving furiously as I respond silently to my best friend's objections, but she's been around me for years and can keep track of my signing with no trouble at all.

"Exactly. Let's just go."

"No. I need this to be finished. Then I can move on, look for another Dom to train me. Maybe Angela will hear of someone else…"

"God, I hope not. If they're all as scary as… Which one is he, anyway? They both look deadly."

"The one nearest us, cream shirt."

"Pity. The other guy's better looking. If you're going to be dropping your pants for a guy, and then let him—whatever—it helps if he's gorgeous, I suppose. Sort of softens the blow, so to speak. Are you sure yours is the cream shirt?"

"Yes. I'm sure. And mine's definitely the most gorgeous. Yours is okay I suppose…"

"Mine? No way. I value my hide too much, and these guys—what did you say they were? Doms?"

I nod helpfully.

"Yeah, well, they just terrify me. And if you'd any sense, you'd be running for the hills now, and not even contemplate marching up to him. Please, Freya, you don't have to do this. If being a member of this weird club is so important to you, why not just buy the place and award yourself life membership?"

"Because that's not the way we do things."

We? We submissives that would be. And for a submissive to contemplate buying a BDSM club and taking charge, in direct defiance of the most powerful Dominant in the place, is so unsubmissive as to be laughable. I shake my head, knowing I can't come close to making Summer understand the complex protocols at play here. Suffice it to say, I have to accept my punishment if I want to move on and be allowed to continue to explore my sexual preferences in the relative security of this safe environment. I turn back to her, and decide to make one last attempt at reassurance.

"I do. I really do. It'll be all right. Afterwards. And I'm grateful to you for coming with me, but you don't need to stay. I know you hate it here. Grab a taxi, I'll pay for it, and I'll see you tomorrow."

"I'm going nowhere. I'll wait for you, and make sure you get home. When he's done with you."

"That won't be necessary. Really." Although I'm doing my best to exude confidence, in truth, I'm not at all sure what state I'll be in by the time Nicholas Hardisty is 'done with me', but I've never yet heard of an instance when a Dom punished a submissive so severely she—or he—was incapable of making their way home. I doubt I'm going to be the first. And however pissed off with me he might be, Nicholas Hardisty is a responsible Dom. He'll hurt me, but he won't go too far. Probably.

Mr Hardisty has his back to me. He's at the bar in the main lounge at the club, leaning casually on the polished surface chatting to his friend, the one Summer seems so taken with, who I vaguely recognize. I think I've heard he's called Daniel, and although not in my opinion nearly as attractive as Nicholas Hardisty, he does seem quite nice. He's always polite to submissives, but I've never scened with him. I've scened with hardly anyone, in fact. Both men are wearing black denim jeans, the normal 'uniform' for Doms as far as I can see, but Mr Hardisty is wearing a casual cream-colored sports shirt in contrast to his companion's more austere black silk shirt. And Mr Hardisty is definitely the more handsome of the two, gorgeous and sexy and so, so hot. I'd say he's in his early thirties, maybe a little older, dark brown hair, slightly over-long perhaps, a little over six feet tall and with shoulders that fill out that sports shirt very nicely indeed.

I know I messed up, contacting him out of the blue like that. Totally messed up. But no one could honestly blame me for wanting Nicholas Hardisty. All the subs want Nicholas Hardisty, but he's very, very selective. The only sub I can ever recall seeing him with—and then only once or twice in all the months I've been watching him here—is a tall, willowy blonde, name of Gina, I think. He doesn't usually indulge himself, at least not here, but I know he's a mentor for several less-experienced Doms. Indeed, my own friend, mentor, and now my champion it seems, Mistress Angela, speaks highly of his skills as a trainer and educator of new subs.

I can see now that I should never have taken matters into my own hands, even though there's no way at all he would ever have noticed me otherwise, the quiet little mouse in the corner. I'm not pretty, not the sort of sub to attract the attention of a sexy, experienced Master like Nicholas Hardisty, not tall and willowy, and definitely not blonde. I definitely shouldn't have offered him money to train me. It never occurred to me that he'd take my approach so amiss, but he did, and I'm lucky to still be here. I owe that to Ange who persuaded him to re-consider, to relent and settle for a physical punishment instead of just throwing me out of the club for good.

Which brings me back to my current dilemma. His instructions were to make myself known to him in order that he could mete out the discipline I seem to require. He laughs, the sound rich, low and incredibly sensual. I sigh. If it weren't for the nature of our coming encounter, he'd seem quite approachable. Almost.

I take a deep breath, squeeze Summer's hand in one last gesture of reassurance then straighten my short black skirt. I adjust the neckline on my cut-off scarlet and black top, before moving silently in his direction. Silently, the way I do everything. Always silent, rarely noticed. And now I'm right behind him, and still he's unaware of my presence. Which creates another pressing problem for me—how to attract his attention? I could simply tap him on the arm, but even as inexperienced as I am, I know a submissive can't just march up and touch a strange Dom without permission. That's definitely not allowed. I could try to clear my throat, but I suspect the sound—if I did indeed manage to make a sound—would just be ridiculous. I don't want him to find me a figure of fun on top of everything else. I'm standing there, uncertain, trying not to fidget, or worse still turn and run, when Daniel saves the day for me. He spots me hovering awkwardly and leans around Mr Hardisty to find out what I'm doing there. His expression is distinctly surprised, no doubt at my temerity in interrupting them.

"Yes?" His tone is stern but icily polite.

Nicholas Hardisty turns to see what the interruption is, and our eyes meet. Briefly. I smile quickly, nervously, before dropping my gaze. I bow slightly, the only ready way I have of expressing respect to a nonsigner, before I step back to a more respectful distance.

"Can we help you?" Daniel again, now regarding me with a somewhat puzzled expression.

I can't blame him really. Submissives just don't walk up to Doms deep in conversation and interrupt, it's not how we do things.

"We're not looking to play just yet, but if we want you, we'll call you over." He glances up, catches sight of Summer hovering a few yards away, and returns his gaze to me. "Both of you, perhaps." Despite his dismissive words, he's polite to me at least, not all Doms would be. He turns away, ready to get back to his conversation with Mr Hardisty, but his companion is still regarding me closely.

"Miss Stone?" His voice is low, controlled, quite formal.

I glance up and nod briefly before lowering my gaze again. Long moments pass, I can feel his eyes on me, assessing me. And no doubt finding me less than enticing, but he has a score to settle, a reputation to uphold. There's no doubt I'm going to be getting my just deserts this evening, though I don't suppose he'll want to waste too much of his time on me. So I stand and wait.

Mr Hardisty turns back to the bar and with a gesture calls the staff member over, a young man called David, I think. He converses with him quickly, his tone low. I peek up and catch the look of surprise on his companion's face. Daniel turns his attention back to me, scrutinizing me much more carefully this time, no doubt keen to discern some hidden allure he may have missed the first time he glanced in my direction. There's speculation undisguised in his gaze, but on further reflection, further careful consideration, he clearly remains less than impressed. He shrugs, shakes his head slightly and turns away from me.

Mr Hardisty concludes his business with David and turns to me, raises his hand to beckon me to him. I approach and stand before him, acutely aware of my diminutive five foot four as he towers over me. I can't drag my eyes from his right hand—I know I'm going to become intimately acquainted with it quite soon and I wonder how many strokes he has in mind. How severe a spanking have I earned?

"I've reserved room nine, upstairs. Please go there and wait for me."

My speculation is interrupted by his voice, his instructions are curt and clipped. He turns away, doesn't see me nod briefly, the flash of relief perhaps evident as I realize I'm not to be subjected to a public humiliation after all. I make my way toward the exit. He doesn't need to see me leave, he knows I'll obey him. Submissives always obey Mr Hardisty.

I stop only long enough to hug Summer, tell her one last time that she really doesn't need to hang around waiting for me, and a couple of minutes later I'm slipping through the door of room nine on the upper floor.

The ground floor at the club is where the public and communal rooms are, the bar, the various lounges and of course my personal favorite—though only ever as a spectator—the dungeon. Members who prefer their activities to be played out in a more secluded setting can make use of the private rooms on the second floor. Some of these are themed, for example one is styled to resemble a classroom and another a nursery for the age regressionists among our number. On one memorable occasion, I was invited to scene with a Dom who had a fetish for curvy little girls in gymslips and no underwear. He enjoyed himself for a while laying stripes across my bottom with a ruler, and I confess I didn't mind that. Not really, if it was going to lead to some more sensual fun later. I was distinctly moist and eagerly anticipating the next phase of our interlude together by the time he was ready to move on. But he wanted to cane my hands as well, and I let him do that too. Then he simply thanked me, said I was a good girl after all, and left to fuck someone else—presumably a bad girl.

I talk with my hands, and he hurt them. They hurt for days. I was truly silenced as well as disappointed and frustrated. I love to sew, and I couldn't do that either for the best part of a week. I expect—hope—Mr Hardisty will be able to demonstrate a little more sensitivity, his reputation certainly suggests that he might. I doubt any submissive ever left his company disappointed and frustrated. Not that I'm his sub exactly. I'm more in the way of an annoyance, a chore, a score to be settled.

I'm relieved to find that room nine is the 'standard' type, exactly like most of the other private rooms here at the Collared and Tied, simply furnished with a spanking bench, a straight backed wooden chair and a double bed in one corner. The shelves and display cases house a range of equipment and toys—whips, canes, a generous supply of spankers and floggers. The walls and ceiling sport an interesting variety of metal loops and anchor points, designed to secure a sub in whatever position is required. There are an impressive selection of vibrators, dildos and nipple clamps as well, but I know that many Doms prefer to use their own stuff. And of course, a drawer containing hundreds of condoms. I doubt somehow that we'll be getting through many of those. Chance would indeed be a very fine thing.

In the absence of any more detailed instructions regarding any preparations I should make, I settle for perching nervously on the edge of the bed. I gaze around me, my eyes returning repeatedly to the chair in the center of the room. Will he opt to sit on that, place me across his knees? I hope so, that seems less clinical somehow. More intimate, offering more direct contact. Will he want me to strip? Doms usually like their submissives to be naked or as near as makes no difference. But Mr Hardisty is not just a Dom, he's a Master. He has a reputation for being hard, firm, strict.

He sets rules and enforces them relentlessly. I broke his rules without even knowing what they were. And now, I have no idea at all what to expect from him.

Except, I know it's going to be painful. Very painful. And despite the club's insistence on safe and consensual play, I have no reliable way of safe wording. Up to now I've relied on the dungeon master to keep an eye out for me, and he's been very attentive. But Frank isn't here in room nine right now, and Mr Hardisty is a stranger. He doesn't know me, doesn't understand me. He might not intend to harm me, but how will he be able to help it? Christ, what have I done?

He makes me wait. And wait. My panic growing, building, my fears whirling around my head as my imagination gets to work and runs riot, twisting me and tying me in knots. I'm confused, terrified and excited in equal parts. I was so keen to meet Nicholas Hardisty, to scene with him. I wanted him to train me — I still do, desperately. But he's refused. Turned me down flat. He won't even discuss it with me. This — whatever I'm to have this evening, is all the help I'm likely to get from him. And I know I'm on thin ice, he could easily rescind my membership again if he decides I'm unsuitable for this club. I can't risk that, I really can't, so I won't be repeating my request. There must be others who could help me. But they're not as highly recommended and for some reason I do want Nicholas Hardisty. No one else appeals.

He's here. The door opens and he's here, in the same room as me, alone with me. All I ever wanted. And the one man, the one Dom, I'm most afraid of. I drop my eyes immediately. My hands, my expressive speaking hands, are twisting together incoherently in my lap. Should I be standing? Kneeling? He remains motionless, watching me, leaning against the door that he clicked quietly closed behind him as he came in. I can feel his eyes on me, assessing me, waiting for me to…what? Oh, Christ, what if I've annoyed him again…? I start to rise, lift my hands ready to start signing an apology.

"Stay there. We need to talk."

His voice stills me. *Talk! Yeah, right. I do a lot of that.*

He comes forward and, grabbing the chair from the middle of the room, drags it toward the bed. He turns it and sits, straddling the seat, his arms folded, elbows lying along the top of the chair back. And he watches me again. He's waiting, waiting for me to say something perhaps. I glance up at him, eye contact and expression are essential tools of communication for me, and I quickly sign an apology. He won't understand my gestures, but it serves as a reminder that I can't speak to him out loud.

"What is that? British Sign Language?" His tone is low, measured. He doesn't sound angry, or irritated.

I nod my reply, and drop my hands uselessly back into my lap.

"Sorry, I don't understand it. So, no vocal sounds at all I think you said in your email?"

I nod then shake my head, not sure how best to respond. He seems to get my meaning though.

"Right. We do need to talk though. Will this do?" He leans over, and pulls his iPhone from his back jeans pocket. He taps the screen a couple of times to bring up a notepad app then holds it out to me.

I gape at him, surprised, and he jerks his hand to remind me to reach out, accept it from him. I'm stunned, I never expected this, didn't expect anything in the way of effort on his part to help me communicate. His face is serious, not especially encouraging, but his actions are speaking volumes to me already. I was so right to select him as my trainer. If only he'd agree.

"I have some questions for you. I require answers. Honest answers, full answers. Do you understand?"

I nod once more, not sure what he might need to ask me. I thought our business was concluded, all except this last episode which really requires no conversation at all beyond 'get undressed and bend over'. Now, it just needs to be got over with.

"Okay. I want you to write your responses down for me. Take your time, we're in no hurry. I want to be absolutely sure though that we understand each other before we're done here." He pauses, watching my reactions closely. He hasn't instructed me to drop my gaze, indeed, I don't think I could if he did require it. His eyes are mesmerizing, deep and dark, slate gray. Beautiful eyes, but so stern, so uncompromising, drilling into mine.

"Why are you here?"

His first question throws me completely. Why *am* I here? I'm here because he bloody well told me to come here, I'm here to be punished, disciplined, my behavior corrected. *What sort of a question's that?* My confusion must be apparent on my face because he chuckles, the sound low and sexy.

"Yes, yes, you're here for a spanking and you'll get that. All in good time. But what I want to know is, why do you deserve to be spanked?"

I shake my head slightly, shrugging, bewildered.

He tilts his head, his expression firming, all trace of humor gone in an instant. "It's not a trick question, girl, and I expect you to answer me. Now. Don't keep me waiting, and don't make me repeat myself. Write down for me why you deserve to be punished. What did you do that needs to be corrected?" His tone is not menacing, not yet threatening, but I know he won't take kindly to having to ask me again.

I try to think, but to be fair my brain is turning into a sort of soggy porridge. This conversation, his question, is so left field, so totally unexpected. I stare at the small screen in my hands, my mind a blank. Obviously I use notepads a lot, electronic and the paper type, in shops that sort of thing. BSL is not widely used or understood so I have to make do. Shopping's easier now that supermarkets have those DIY checkouts, but still…

I write down the first thing that occurs to me.

I broke the rules of being a submissive by making contact with a Dominant, before I was invited to?

I hand the phone back to Nicholas Hardisty who reads my short response rapidly before passing it straight back.

"Nice try. That would have earned you a reprimand, not a spanking. Think again, girl. And this time don't try to evade, I think you know what your offense was. But I intend to make sure you understand what all this is about before we proceed."

I take the phone and stare at it for a few moments. It must have been the money. Angela warned me against offering to pay, but I still did it. Idiot that I am, I should have listened. That must be it. I insulted him by offering him money. Still, it might be worth trying one more possibility.

I invited a Dominant to scene with me, when the invitation should have come from him. I should have waited until I was asked.

Again I hand him the phone, and once more he glances briefly at it before passing it back to me.

"Last chance, girl. And just in case you're in any doubt, you're pissing me off and wasting my time. You have five seconds to start being honest with me and then I'm going to suspend you from that ring in the ceiling above your pretty but empty little head, strip you and take a strap to your delicious little arse until I do get the truth out of you. Am I making myself clear here?"

He is, and I'm suitably terrified now, I nod. It was the money, had to be. And he's not letting up. Unless I want my punishment to suddenly get a whole lot worse, I need to give him the honest answer he's demanding. I take the phone again, and start to type.

I offered you money if you'd agree to be my Dom, to train me.

I hand back the phone, he glances at it, then his eyes flick back to me. This time he doesn't fling it back at me.

"Bingo." His softly uttered word is more intimidating than any curse, insult or threat might have been. He looks at me, long and hard, his eyes quite glacial. "Now we're getting somewhere at last. And why, girl, was that wrong? Why do you suppose that's gotten you into such a lot of trouble?"

I look up and shrug. His expression hardens, darkens. He thinks I'm being dismissive, defiant even, making light of this. *Christ!* I snatch the phone back from him, not especially submissive or polite, but I'm desperate now, and very, very scared. I have to make him understand. I start to tap out my message quickly, panicking, frantic.

Please, I don't know. I really don't. I'm not being rude or difficult. Please don't…

Suddenly he reaches out, covers my hand with his and stops my frenetic tapping. "Look at me, girl." His voice is soft now, he expects me to obey him, but his tone is more reassuring than intimidating.

I lift my gaze, caught in those stormy gray eyes of his again. "I was angry for a moment and I'd no right to be. I insulted you and I threatened you. I'm sorry about that. It was my fault, not yours. I'll always give you time to explain, to ask questions, to understand. You don't need to be worried that not being able to speak to me will earn you a punishment. Lying to me will, evading my questions will. But if you're telling me the truth, you've no need to be afraid of me."

Wide-eyed I place the phone on my lap and wait for him to explain further. He doesn't. We sit, in silence, each of us waiting, for—what?

"If you have a question for me please write it down." Nicholas Hardisty breaks the silence. "If you don't have any questions, then please just write down why offering me money was such a bad idea, why it got you banned from the club at first, and then brought you here for me to spank you instead. And, girl, please hurry up. We're making a lot of progress, but I do want to be getting on with my evening. But first I intend to teach you a lesson you will not be forgetting. Ever."

I do have questions. Lots of questions. The problem is I've no idea at this precise moment just what they might be. So instead I settle for stabbing around in the dark again. I start to write.

I insulted you. By offering to pay you.

I hand back the phone.

He glances at it, nods briefly. "Yes, that's part of it. But I'm a big boy, I'd survive an insult from a little sub like you. That would've earned you a reprimand, maybe a spanking but nothing too heavy. But you're here for a punishment beating. I'm going to really hurt you. Now why is that, do you suppose?" His voice is soft, quiet, but the core thread of determined steel is there, lacing his words.

I offered you too much money. You said it was too much.

Again he reads, nods briefly. "As you pointed out, though, how you spend your money is your choice, not mine. If you want to throw it about, that's up to you."

The phone is back in my hands, and now I'm genuinely at a loss, I don't have a clue what else to say, what else to write down. I feel helpless and scared, utterly rigid with fear. Tears are pricking the backs of my eyes, but pride alone prevents them from falling…yet. I glance up at the ring in the ceiling and despite his reassurance just now, I know I can't avoid what's coming. I don't even have a safe word to fall back on, to get me out of this. I'm so out of my depth, there's something massive here and I just can't see it, just don't get it.

"If you have a question for me, please write it down and I'll try to answer you." Again that cool, calm, firm voice. The voice of authority, demanding obedience.

What *is* my question? God knows, but I settle for writing down the only thing in my head. It takes a couple of minutes, my hands are shaking, but he's patient, he doesn't hurry me or try to read my response before I hand it to him.

I don't know. I really, really don't know. Sir. I never meant to offend you. I wanted you to help me, so much. I was sure you could and I just didn't think you'd do it for nothing. I'm truly sorry. Please, just punish me as you see fit now and let me go. Please. I'm sorry. I'd answer you if I could, you have to believe that.

I chew my bottom lip and twist my fingers together while he reads my frantic note. He thinks there's more, I know he does. And he's already told me he's quite prepared to beat the truth out of me. Well, good luck to him. I just know that the moment he suspends me from the ceiling—if he does—I'm going to simply faint. There'll be no 'truth' to be had out of me. Or maybe I'll just die of fear. Is it possible to actually die of fear?

"I do believe you. You can relax, at least for a few minutes, while I explain."

I look at him, startled. He actually believes me. Wow. I told him the truth and he *did* believe it.

He smiles slightly, amused at my astonishment. "Over the years I've gotten quite good at knowing when a sub's lying, holding back. You were at first, but not now. I can see that. Even without words I can see how frightened you are. Your eyes are telling me that. You do have very expressive eyes, Miss Stone. And here, this evening, I want you to be scared, so scared you can taste it. *Can* you taste it, little sub?"

I nod, my tears falling freely now, well beyond any attempt at subterfuge or false bravado.

"Good, because the fear you're experiencing now might, just might, be the last time you ever need to feel like this. If you listen to me and learn from what I'm going to tell you—and what I'm going to do to you. So, are you ready to learn, Miss Stone?" His head is cocked to one side as he regards me casually, he might as well have just asked if I take milk and sugar for all the impact this conversation is having on him.

I'm shaking so hard I'm no longer able to hold the precious phone. It falls to the floor with a clatter. Nicholas Hardisty leans down and picks it up, places it beside me on the bed. Then he turns back to me, catches my gaze and, without words, I know I'm not to look away.

"You offered me money. A lot of money. You offered twenty-five thousand pounds to a perfect stranger. You'd no way of knowing I wouldn't just take your cash, maybe knock you around a bit, then run."

At my start of protest, he holds up one finger, instantly stilling me.

"I know, I came recommended. By Angela. Did you know Ange is my sister?" He shakes his head wryly. "No, by your expression I guess you didn't. We could have been in it together, maybe we planned to share your money. You were just plain gullible, Miss Stone, a poor little rich kid with more money than sense. Christ, you're not fit to be let out, girl."

I stare at him, my heart sinking, despairing, utterly crushed. He's right. Of course he's right. What a fool, what a stupid, naïve little fool. And the worst of it is, I really did trust Mistress Angela. She's been kind to me, always. Firm, but fair and caring. And now he's telling me she was just using me, cheating me. I can't believe it, was I really so stupid, so easily taken in? Surely I couldn't have been so completely fooled, I've known her for months now, she knows me, understands how hard it is for me sometimes... The disappointment, the sense of betrayal is more painful than anything else.

He smiles, takes pity perhaps on my stricken expression. "Don't look so distraught, your instincts about Angela were right. She's on your side and was never out for anything but your best interests. And I gather she did advise you against offering to pay me?"

I nod, at least that bit of logic makes sense and I can hang onto some shred of sanity in all this. Mistress Angela can't have been after my money if she didn't want me to put any on the table. She did advise me not to offer to pay, just to ask nicely. It was my idea, only mine, to put a price tag on Nicholas Hardisty. And look where it got me.

"And what did you think you'd be buying with your twenty-five thousand pounds? A trip to Alton Towers?"

He picks up the phone and pulls up his emails, finds mine from all those weeks ago. He starts to read from it, "'...*work with me, train me in order that I can become accustomed to submission and the BDSM lifestyle. I am interested in exploring the various forms of submission, the usual and most common practices, and so on'*." He stops, looks up at me, disdain and dismissal all over his face. "A D/s relationship is not a trip to a bloody theme park, and a trainer is a lot more than a fucking tour guide. What did you think I'd do, take you around, show you the sights, give you a pack of sandwiches and make sure you were back on your bus well in time for your evening meal?"

He's glaring at me now, contempt etched firmly across his handsome face, his slate eyes glittering. If I could feel any smaller I'd probably disappear down a crack in the floorboards. I'm sobbing now, really sobbing, but it's my own brand of silent weeping. Unable to bear his intense, accusing, disgusted gaze any longer, I cover my face with my hands, my shoulders heaving as I continue to sob, just desperate now to be done with this and allowed to crawl away somewhere, anywhere. To hide, to hate myself as much as he seems to. To try to forget I ever imagined I could do any of this. I hear the chair creak as he gets up.

"Well, if that's all the sense I'm going to get out of you, we might as well finish this now. Stand up and get undressed." His tone is clipped, distant, he just wants to be done with me and get away, back to much more interesting and worthwhile companions.

And miserable though I am, humiliated and cowed under the weight of his distaste, I gather together some residual shreds of self-worth, enough to make my last protest, my last appeal for some sort of bloody justice in all this. I grab the phone, now lying beside me on the bed once more. He said he'd always give me time if I've something to say—well now I have, and he can bloody well wait.

I know I need help. I know I need to learn. I want to learn. I asked you to help me. I was wrong about the money and I'm sorry. I messed up. Badly. And I know you won't help me now. But I still need to be trained. Please, is there anyone else I can ask?

I thrust the iPhone back at him. While he's reading I do as he's instructed me to do. I stand and remove my cropped top. I'm braless underneath, naturally, and in a show of defiance—dwindling but still flickering faintly—I turn my back on him as I start to unfasten the zip at the side of my miniskirt. Under that I have a thong. He might make me remove that too—just because he can—even though it offers me no protection apart from to my modesty. But he'll have to bloody well tell me.

"Sit down again, Miss Stone. It seems we're not through talking yet." His tone is less formal, slightly warmer.

I hesitate, reach for my discarded top intending to pull it back on.

"No, leave that. And turn around—I want to look at you." His tone brooks no argument as he puts a stop to any notion of modesty, meager though it would be.

I turn, and with some not inconsiderable effort manage to tilt my chin up and meet his gaze as I once more sit on the edge of the bed. Nicholas Hardisty is no longer straddling the chair, he's leaning casually against the spanking bench, his arms folded, his iPhone in his right hand. He taps it against his left elbow, watching me thoughtfully. His eyes drop to my breasts and I resist the urge to cover myself. I draw some comfort from the fact that I have nice boobs. Well I think so. I only wear a size thirty-four bra, but I'm a curvy C cup. Nipples a little on the small side maybe, to the ungenerous eye, but with some careful attention… The look of appreciation in Nicholas Hardisty's eyes suggests he's not about to quarrel with my self-assessment. But still, he makes me wait.

At last, he speaks to me again. "A D/s relationship is a contract, sure enough, but it's not a financial one. And it's not a series of experiences, something for thrill-seekers to spice up their sex lives with. Nothing wrong with that, of course, the occasional bit of kink to keep things interesting, but a BDSM lifestyle, a Dom/sub relationship, now that's a whole lot more." He strolls toward me, stops in front of me, then, amazingly, he crouches before me, looking up at me now. Our relative positions reversed, he goes on, his tone low and soft and incredibly gentle, "Submission, Miss Stone, is a state of mind. You give a Dom your submission because he's earned it. You give it freely and willingly, it's not a commodity to be bought or sold."

I make to reach for the phone, but he stills me again, just by raising a finger. Christ, the power in that raised finger — I can see his Dominant qualities plainly in that gesture. It doesn't matter that he's placed himself lower than me, that he's looking up at me, there's no doubt whatsoever who's in charge here. And he hasn't finished yet.

"I know you were trying to buy, not sell, but the principle's the same. Do you see that?"

He waits, and I nod, hesitant, but I am beginning to see what he's getting at.

He continues with his explanation. "And I'm not for sale either. If I ever do decide to put my time into training a submissive, it'll be because I like her, respect her, see potential in her and want to help bring it out. Not because she paid me a fucking great pile of money to show her the sights. And believe me, Miss Stone, any Dom who'd take your money is not one you want to learn from."

He stops, his eyes on mine, his gaze intent. He reaches up, takes my chin in his palm, holds my face still, connecting with me. He waits for a few moments, lets his words sink in. Then, "Is that all perfectly clear, Miss Stone? Do you understand now why your proposition would never work? It's not a matter of telling you who else to approach. You need to give this up. Give it up now. Not everyone's cut out for this lifestyle of ours. Submission needs to be in you, a good Dom can train you, develop your nature, hone your innate talents. But I think you're a fairground rider, Miss Stone, a thrill seeker. My advice to you is to just have fun from time to time, but leave the serious stuff to others better suited to it."

He's wrong. Wrong about me, I know it. I frown, shake my head, but he's said all he's going to say, given me all the free tuition I'm going to get it seems. He stands, towering over me as I continue to sit on the edge of the bed, drowning in bitter frustration that he can't—won't—see beyond my clumsy inexperience to discover the potential beneath. The deep commitment, a yearning I can never remember not feeling. I won't be giving up. I'll never give up. I clench my fists, draw in a deep breath. I've lost this battle, I can see that. So now, time to end it.

I stand, return to unzipping my skirt and drop it on the floor. I make no move to remove my thong, and he lets that be, just a slight quirk of his lips to show he's registered my defiance. Oddly enough, I feel much less afraid of his anger now. I know he'll control it. Somehow. Despite my lack of any safe words, he'll still manage not to go too far. Instinctively, I'm feeling safe. Well, almost safe.

"I have a present for you, Miss Stone."

He slips his hand into his jeans pocket and pulls out two silicon wristbands, the sort you buy to give money to charities or to show support for a cause. I still have my white *Make Poverty History* wristbands in a drawer at home. These ones are plain though, no snappy slogans, and one is a vivid crimson red color, the other yellow. He holds them out to me, in his palm.

"Give me your left hand."

Puzzled, I hold out my hand and he slips the red wristband onto it.

"Now your right."

I hold out my other hand, and he slips the yellow band onto that.

"You're left-handed, yes?"

I nod. He must have noticed which hand I used to type my notes on his phone.

"Okay. Red means 'stop', 'enough', 'no more'. That's your safe word for this. Or safe signal, I suppose. You've only to raise your left hand, the one with the red wristband, and that stops everything, immediately, no questions. The yellow band means 'slow down', 'not sure', 'need to talk'. Does that sound okay to you? It's crude, I know, but can we manage with that?"

I'm stunned. Yet again he's astounded me just by thinking ahead and having a plan in place to help me communicate. First the phone, now this. Bemused, I nod, then suddenly think of something, a problem. I place my hands behind my back, as they would be if I was tied, and I shrug. Nicholas Hardisty smiles, shakes his head. "Ah, but I won't be tying you up, Miss Stone. And you'll be on the bench where I can easily see your hands. If you signal, if you need me to stop, I *will* see you. And I *will* stop." He pauses, then, his voice soft, he continues, "Look at me, Miss Stone, and understand this. I would never, ever lay a hand on a sub—let alone lay her across a spanking bench and take a paddle to her arse—hard—unless I was absolutely certain I knew her safe word, and that she was free and able to use it. You *will* be safe with me. So, now you know exactly what's in store for you, are you ready to start?"

No alternative now, no further discussion, nothing else for it. So I just dip my head. Nicholas Hardisty moves aside, gestures toward the spanking bench. "Lean across the top, stretch your upper body along the bench and reach your hands out as far in front of you as you can."

I walk over to the bench, slowly, but not so slowly that he could take issue and maybe find a reason to force the pace a little. I'd really prefer to take my time over this. Then I remember my yellow wristband, my 'slow down' signal. I can ask for more time if I need it. And suddenly I realize how totally liberating that simple fact now is. I can even put a stop to this whole thing, just by raising my left hand, exerting the power of the red band. I'm not helpless, I have an escape route. If I take this beating from Mr Hardisty, it's because I've decided to allow it, to accept it from him, not because I had no choice. Now, here with Nicholas Hardisty, I can choose to submit.

I stop, look down at my two wrists, and glance back over my shoulder at Mr Hardisty. He's watching me intently, and seems to know the instant the penny drops. He winks at me. The mighty Dom actually winks. And I do something incredible too, something I'd never have thought I could even contemplate doing. Ever. I turn to him, and I run at him. I throw my arms around him and I hug him. His arms close around me briefly before I step back, sedately, and offer him my hand to shake. Sensitive as well as powerful, my gesture of gratitude is not lost on Nicholas Hardisty. He takes my hand, nods to me politely, his softly murmured "You're welcome" proving beyond any doubt that he gets it. Gets me. Then, it's back to the business in hand.

"Now, little wannabe sub, on the bench please. Let's see what you're made of."

Chapter Two

"Do you want to see the paddle I intend to use?" The cool, matter-of-fact voice is coming from right alongside me.

He's very close, I can feel him, the whisper of his jeans, the movement of air as he positions himself.

I shake my head, pressing my face into the buttery soft leather padding on the top of the spanking bench. I'm already positioned, have been for the last few minutes as he's once more taken his time and made me wait. I'm lying face down, bent at the waist, my feet on the floor and my upper body pressed into the leather. It feels warm against my naked breasts, not unpleasant at all. Just—strange. My arms are outstretched and I'm gripping the far end of the bench tightly. Under clear and direct instructions not to move, I'm acutely conscious of my bare buttocks, exposed and vulnerable, the rear string of the thong my only passing nod at modesty. And all the time I've been listening, listening to Nicholas Hardisty moving about the room, listening to him opening one of the cabinets, then another one, obviously selecting which items he intends to use tonight. On me.

"In that case, I insist that you *do* look. Open your eyes, little sub."

I frown, shake my head again, quickly. Why can't he just get on with it, get it over with, and let me go?

"That was not a request, and I won't tell you again." His tone is hard, firm, implacable.

I have no choice but to obey. He's standing to my right when I open my eyes and find myself staring at a point just below his belt buckle, not more than six inches from my face. From what I can see, he has an erection, quite impressive, and I'm glad about that, it shows he's not unmoved by my naked presence spread out before him. He lets me look my fill for a few moments before stepping back. He was holding the paddle behind his back while I ogled his erect cock, but now he brings it around, holding it loosely between his two hands.

"Have you felt one of these before? On your bare arse, obviously?"

I look at the instrument, gulping a little—it looks huge. And weighty. I shake my head.

"This one's made of rubber. It's quite flexible, and it's heavy. It delivers a sharp sting, very painful while it's being applied, but the pain won't last long afterwards. You'll be able to walk out of here a few minutes later. You're quite small, delicate build, and this particular paddle is at the top end of what you might be able to stand. But this is a punishment beating, you know that. It's meant to hurt. I won't be gentle with you, but I'll do you no lasting damage either. You *will* struggle, especially toward the end, but you should be able to cope. And you have your wristbands—use them if you need to."

He strolls around to the other side of the bench, and I follow him with my eyes, turning my face to keep him in sight. He stops by my left shoulder and I can feel his eyes raking along my body, assessing. At last, he pronounces his judgment. "You have a pretty little body, Miss Stone, curvy and soft. A little on the small side, perhaps, but still very pretty. And you'll look even prettier when I've brought out the delicate reds and pinks in your sweet little bum cheeks. You'll be receiving twenty strokes…"

I flinch—twenty! With that huge paddle! I'd thought maybe twelve at most. He sees, smiles wryly.

"Twenty in total. The first ten with my hand, to prepare you a little. I won't be gentle, but it will give you a chance to get your head together, get used to feeling the pain, riding it, breathing through it. Then the final ten with the paddle. And I want you to hold the paddle please, until I'm ready for it."

The sadist. The cruel bastard is really rubbing the salt in. He makes me release my grip on the edge of the bench and instead wrap my fingers around the handle and the blade of the black rubber monster he's selected. Apparently satisfied at last that I'm as terrified as he can conceivably achieve, no more words are spoken as he moves down to stand behind me. I brace, waiting for the first blow to fall, and almost leap off the bench as his palm connects with my left buttock. But it's not a slap, it's a caress.

"Keep still, I won't tell you again." His tone is firm, stern now as he reprimands me. "I don't intend to tie your hands, but I will strap you in place around the waist and the knees if I need to. Now, I just want to make sure your circulation is stimulated, get some blood to the surface of your skin, help you to fully appreciate what I have to offer you. Would you like to thank me for my kindness, Miss Stone?"

I concentrate on remaining perfectly still, but apparently that's not enough now.

"Miss Stone, pay attention. I asked you a question. Would you like to thank me for my kindness? You can answer by nodding. Or not."

Discretion is without doubt the better part of valor. I nod.

"Good, you're learning. Now, you should feel free to enjoy this part if you like."

He continues to caress and massage my bum, digging his finger ends into the fleshy cheeks, sliding them under my thong to trace the crack between my buttocks, even circling my most private little orifice with one gentle fingertip. I manage to remain still, but can't help the little gasp which escapes me. In the silence of the room it sounds like a steam train. "Are you very sensitive here, Miss Stone?" He helpfully probes my tight sphincter once more, just to make sure I know where he means. "Or maybe just shy?"

Rhetorical question? I've no idea—not sure if, or how, to answer. He helps me out of my dilemma again.

"Yellow for sensitive and you want me to be careful, red for shy and you want me to stop. Which is it, Miss Stone?"

I hesitate for just a moment before raising my left hand, the red wristband. No point in anything less than an honest response, no one has ever explored my bum before and I'm not at all sure I like it. I'm definitely acutely embarrassed but much, much too intimidated to move or even think about asking him to stop. But he does stop even so, and I realize that I used the 'red' signal. Was that why he stopped? Was that my first little practice at safe wording? His way of demonstrating to me that it works?

I'm still pondering that mystery when the first blow lands, full, hard and sharp across my left buttock, and I jerk on the bench, His hand is heavy, the slap reverberating around the room. He waits a couple of seconds before landing the next one, this time on my right buttock. Again I jerk—it hurts, really hurts. My knuckles are white as I grip the paddle, grinding my teeth to bear the pain. The third slap falls on my left buttock again, followed closely by another to the right. I'm shaking now, only sheer force of his will keeping me in place. I know if I move it'll be worse in the long run.

Just take it, survive it.

"Don't fight it, absorb it. Breathe slowly, in before I slap you, and out afterwards." His tone is calm and measured, his advice no doubt perfectly sound.

Even so my first, inner reaction is along the lines of 'Fuck you, you sadistic bastard'.

The next slap is harder than the first four were.

"More respect, please, Miss Stone. Now, breathe in and out slowly, it *will* be easier for you." His near-telepathic reading of my inner thoughts is uncanny.

I bite my lip, my mouth desperately working as I struggle to maintain any sort of calm. Only half way through the so-called easy bit and already my bottom feels to be in flames.

"Listen to me, concentrate." That low, measured timbre again, but it is managing to penetrate my tortured consciousness.

I'm trying to listen, to obey.

"Breathe in slowly…"

I do, or try to, my breath ragged but responding.

"Now, out."

Again, I obey.

"Good, that's it. In, out, in, out…"

Under his direction, I manage to get a grip on my body's reactions, some semblance of control. I open my eyes and see his face, close to mine—he's been crouching alongside me, whispering his instructions into my ear. He smiles briefly at me.

"Five to go. So now, you're going to breathe in, hold it and breathe out when I slap you. And when you breathe out, open and relax your fingers too. Can you try that?"

I manage to nod, and he smiles again before he stands, moves back into position behind me.

"Breathe in, now."

I do, and a couple of seconds later breathe out in response to the slap landing on my right buttock. It hurts, but the endorphins have kicked in now and combine with my steady, deliberate breathing to make it easier to bear. The pain radiates through me, out of me, and is absorbed almost into the bench. My fingers relax, without conscious effort from me.

"Good, now again. Breathe in…"

I obey, and the next four slaps are delivered, absorbed and melt away into the bench. Instead of getting harder, more excruciating, each slap seems easier, more bearable, more…welcome almost, than the one before it. And then he straightens, he's done. Done with this phase anyway. Now for the main event.

"Give me the paddle now, Miss Stone."

Never contemplating for a moment that I might protest or plead, I uncurl my fingers from around it and push it along the bench toward his outstretched hand. He takes it, and in my peripheral vision I can see him flexing it between his hands as he strolls back around to his position behind me.

"Nod when you're ready for me to start, Miss Stone. And remember, your wristbands are there if you need them. If you want me to slow down, give you a few moments to rest, recover, you use the yellow one. If you need to call a halt altogether, it's the red one." He pauses for a moment, then, "You're doing really well, Freya. You *can* do this. Now are you ready?"

I nod, and have the presence of mind to breathe in slowly and deeply before the first blow lands. Then all presence of mind leaves me in a blinding rush of intense pain. This is worse, much worse than anything I could have ever imagined. I forget to breathe in slowly, forget to breathe at all as the next blow lands. And the next two follow, in rapid succession. If I could scream, I'd be screaming now, rattling the walls and lifting the roof with my screams. As it is I grind my teeth, press my body and my face into the soft leather and try to remember how to pray. I can feel my tears soaking into the leather under my cheeks, my face is wet, I'm sobbing soundlessly. I'm gripping the end of the bench, my last desperate hold on consciousness.

"Okay, time out." Nicholas Hardisty has stopped, and a few seconds later he's crouching once more beside me, lifting the hair from my face. He presses the open neck of a bottle of cool water against my mouth. "Drink."

Gratefully, I swallow a few drops of the cool, refreshing water, my throat working frantically. He offers me more, I accept.

"You forgot to use your safe signal. The yellow one, at least. You needed to stop back then, and you should have told me."

I open my eyes again, frown at him, puzzled. Why *did* he stop then...? He sees my confusion, fills in the blanks.

"You were barely conscious. Another stroke and you would have lost consciousness, and then you'd be helpless. I was watching you. I could see you were losing it, and I won't let that happen. A Dom relies on body language as much as on words to know how his sub is feeling. But you have to look after yourself too. Take responsibility for yourself, make your own choices. I've given you the signals, you have to use them, to protect yourself. Do you understand me?"

I stare at him, perplexed, struggling to take it in. Protect myself? Make my own choices? Easy for him to say, when I'm the one lying naked on a bench, beaten almost senseless. His eyes are on mine, the deep, dark gray boring into me, as if he knows what's in my head.

"You're here because you've chosen to be." His words convince me that somehow he does know what I'm thinking. "You consented and you can withdraw that consent at any time. You can stop this whenever you want, you can get up, get dressed and walk away. And you can stop frowning and shaking your head. It's true. And before you ask, no, I won't have your membership here revoked if you safe word before I'm finished with you. If you've genuinely taken all you can, if you've reached your limit and can go no further, then I'll accept that. We'll be done here, this will all be over. Do you want to do that, Miss Stone? Do you want to use your red wristband?"

I regard him for a few more moments, then I amaze myself and perhaps him a little too, as I shake my head. His eyebrows are raised in silent admiration as he nods his approval at me and stands up.

"Good, I'm impressed. Shall we finish this now then?"

Again, I nod. He retrieves his paddle from the floor and once more, he takes up his position. "Six left. Are you ready for me to continue?"

At my quick nod he brings the paddle down again. It hurts again, just as much as before. I try, vainly, to apply the breathing trick, but this is just too much, the pain too intense, too blinding to have any hope of overcoming it, riding or getting above and beyond it. I can only lie there, trust him not to kill me and whimper to myself in silent agony until it's done.

And that's what eventually works. A lifetime later, or was it really just a few seconds, he's dropping the paddle to the floor. To his credit, Nicholas Hardisty doesn't hang around over getting me past the finishing post. He's lifting my hair from my face, pouring cool, refreshing water into my mouth, across my parched lips. I swallow, running my tongue around my dry mouth, only now realizing how arid that inner landscape has become. He holds the bottle to my mouth, encourages me to take more.

Satisfied at last, I push the bottle away, still too feeble, too fragile to move. But as the vicious pain subsides, slowly receding, and I recover the power of coherent thought, I realize he told me the truth. I may have been hurt, temporarily, but I'm basically undamaged. I have survived it, it's gone—my punishment is behind me now. I will walk out of here, just as Nicholas Hardisty promised me.

"Are you able to stand up?" His voice is gentle now, his hand still in my hair, raking it softly back from my face.

My tears are still streaming, my silent sobs still shake my body, I'm still trembling, but I'm quieting.

Starting to relax, to recover. But I'm nowhere near ready to stand under my own steam yet, so I shake my head and cling on to the top of the bench.

"Right then." And with no further ado, Mr Hardisty scoops me up, effortlessly, and carries me the few paces to the bed. He lays me down, gently on my front, and sits alongside me, again stroking my hair.

I like it. I ease my head toward his hand, nestling against his palm.

"You did well, really well. I'm very impressed." His voice is soft, calming me. Reassuring me. "I really thought you'd use that red band, and I wouldn't have blamed you. Twenty was a lot, for a tiny little thing like you. I didn't expect you to be able to take it. You're tougher than you look."

I shudder, the memory of my ordeal still raw. But under the horror is a growing sense of...what? Something else, something different entirely. Pride maybe. Delight that I've pleased him, that I've earned his approval and his admiration. And—achievement. I feel a strong and growing sense of personal satisfaction. I completed my test, I did what I had to do. What I set out to do. My smile is watery, yes, but genuine as I gaze up at him. He's finished with me, he'll be going soon, but I want him to know I'm okay.

And I wish, I wish with every fiber of my shaky little being, that he was mine, that he was my Dom. But he isn't, will never be, he's made that clear. And now, he's going. He'll be leaving me here, on my own.

Sure enough, he gets up, stands over me, looking down at my sore but still rather smug little body.

"You won't want to sit down for a while, and your bottom is a truly gorgeous shade of crimson. Absolutely glowing. If it wasn't against house rules, I'd take a picture to show you later. But still..." He smiles at me again, his arms folded now as he gets ready to leave me.

"I intend to spend the rest of my evening in the dungeon. You, Miss Stone, you have a choice to make. This room is reserved for the rest of the evening, you can stay here as long as you like, as long as you need to. You won't be disturbed. And when you're ready you can either stay and enjoy the rest of your evening at the club, or you can call it a night and go home, it's up to you.

"Or, Miss Stone, you can ask me to wait while you get dressed, and then you can come with me, spend the rest of the evening with me, in the dungeon. Which would you prefer? The red band says you've had enough of me, and want me to fuck off now and leave you alone. Or the yellow tells me to wait for you. Oh, and Miss Stone, one more thing you should know before you choose. If you choose yellow, then we *will* end up back here before the night's over. And I *will* fuck you until you *do* faint. I'll make a good job of it, I promise you that, but if you really don't want to be fucked tonight, hard and long and very, very deep, you need to show me your red wristband now."

I'm staring at him, sure I'm hallucinating. He must have hit me harder than either of us thought. Or I'm out cold and dreaming. Did the wonderful, sexy, gorgeous Nicholas Hardisty, the most adorable, desirable Dom I've ever laid eyes on, did that Nicholas Hardisty really just invite me to scene with him in the dungeon here at the Collared and Tied club, then promise to bring me back here and fuck me till I faint? Did I really hear that? Was he actually talking to me?

Apparently so, because now he's back, crouching alongside me again, his face inches from mine. "Well, Miss Stone, do I stay or do I go?"

I gaze at him, wonderstruck, for a few more moments before I manage to wriggle my arms free from underneath me. And I reach out to him, with my right hand. The yellow band.

Nicholas Hardisty smiles, warm, welcoming, his pleasure genuine. He takes my outstretched hand and turns it palm up, drops a kiss onto the center of my palm. "Good, I'm glad. I'm going to enjoy your company tonight, Miss Stone."

Chapter Three

In true Dom/sub tradition I thought I'd be walking behind him as we make our way down the stairs and along the central corridor in the club. Instead, as we leave room nine Nicholas Hardisty holds out his hand to me. I take it, and find myself walking beside him. At the top of the stairs, he stops to exchange a few words with another Dom, an older man I vaguely recognize, called Richard, I think. When I would have hung back discreetly he tugs me forward, right alongside him and drapes his arm across my shoulders, sinking his fingers into my hair. Telling me I belong here, with him, at least for tonight. So I stay close, soaking it up, drinking it in.

At the door to the dungeon he stops, turns to me, tips my chin up with his finger. "You okay? Still happy to come in here with me?"

I smile and nod.

Happy? This is all my Christmases and birthdays come at once. I never could have imagined this, never could have expected to be here, and as someone's sub. And not just anyone's sub. Nicholas Hardisty's. Wow!

I often spend my time at the *Collar* down here, most of the unattached subs do. But usually, invariably, I'm just watching—the pleasure vicarious at best—a passive audience to the sensual joys and dramas of others. Other subs with regular Doms, perhaps, or the really attractive, popular, better trained subs who are always in demand, can always rely on being invited to join a scene. But I'm inexperienced, and I know I'm hard work. My lack of vocal clues and responses makes me a less rewarding prospect than most other subs. The more responsible Doms are uncertain of my consent because I can't tell them what I want and don't want, and the less responsible ones just scare me. So I usually sit on the edge and settle for watching from the sidelines. But not tonight. Tonight, I could get to play too. If I want to.

We enter the dungeon, Nicholas Hardisty's arm still looped around my shoulders. I catch a ripple of movement from a group of subs just inside the door, over to my right, and I know they've seen, they're speculating about how I came to land this fish. I manage not to look their way, keep my attention focused on my Dom for the evening, remembering my manners. Good manners are essential to a sub, the alternative is to be corrected, punished. And I've taken enough punishment for one night. So now, I'm on my best behavior.

"Would you like a drink? Water? Pepsi? Juice?" Nicholas is smiling at me, obviously pleased with my attitude so far.

I'd very much like an orange juice, but I'm starting to get flustered, wondering how to tell him what I want. He notices, and goes through the options again, but this time holding up the fingers on his left hand, and using his right index finger to point to each one as he names my choices. I smile, delighted, and tap his left index finger, the juice finger.

He nods, holds up two fingers. "Orange, or apple?"

Again he points to indicate the selections, and I tap his finger to indicate orange. Then we go through the same procedure to establish ice or no ice, before Nicholas strolls off to the bar in the corner. He comes back a minute or two later with a tall glass of iced orange juice for me and a glass of what looks to be sparkling water for himself. He hands me my glass, then laces his fingers through mine to lead me farther into the dungeon. I tighten my grip on his hand as I follow him over to an empty couch more or less in the middle of the huge room.

The spot is dark and secluded, but with a good view all around us. He taps his glass against mine, the cheery clink reinforcing his easy, relaxed, undemanding attitude. Gone now is the harsh Dom I had to contend with upstairs, the one who reduced me to tears just with his words, then went on to beat the living daylights out of me. In fairness, in retrospect, it wasn't all bad. He also gave me tools and tricks to help me communicate, to give me choice and a way to protect myself. He took the time and trouble to listen to what I had to say, he answered my questions, helped me to understand this lifestyle choice of ours better than I ever have before. He helped me to see where I'd gone wrong, and he also managed to instil in me the confidence and courage to get me through the worst, most painful discipline I have ever faced. So yes, I have no complaints so far.

That Dom was then, now I have a friendly, warm companion, ready to show me a good time. And I intend to enjoy myself.

"So, you've seen me here before? In the dungeon?"

I look at him, surprised, how did he know I'd been watching him? I always stay out of sight, never draw attention to myself. Don't I?

"In your email. You said you'd seen me here, in the dungeon. Do you spend a lot of time down here?"

I nod, take another sip of my orange juice as he pulls out his phone again. My heart sinks. Am I boring him already? But he hands it to me, the notepad app back on the screen. "So, how come you've seen me, but I can't remember ever seeing you before?"

I look down at the phone in my hand, it's designed for surfing the internet and whatever else, but I suspect he never had this particular use in mind when he bought it. It's simple enough though, if you're used to this sort of thing. I am. I have a similar sort of smart phone, but it's tucked away in my bag in the cloakroom. I even have an app on mine which supposedly converts typed words into speech, but I never use it. I'd rather sign elegantly or write things down than sound like a Dalek with laryngitis and speak at a rate of three words a minute. I quickly tap out my response on the tiny on-screen keyboard.

Only couples and Doms tend to come and sit here, in the middle. I usually stand over there by the door, with the other subs. You'd never see me there. It's too dark.

I hand the phone back to him, he reads quickly, then turns me on the settee so my back is against his side. He puts the phone back in my hands. "Now I can read over your shoulder, as you're writing. So, you usually just watch then?"

I nod, no need to write that.

"What do you watch? What's your favorite sort of scene? Is there anything you'd like to try?"

I hesitate, thinking, not sure. The choices are endless. The possibilities spread out before me seem limitless in this moment, and I have no idea where to settle. He chuckles, tightens his arms around my waist, his fingers spread across my stomach, warm and firm against my bare flesh. "You seem tense, Miss Stone. While you're thinking about that, let me help you to relax." He slides his hand up, under my crop top, cupping and caressing my breast, first the right, then the left.

"Is this okay?" He murmurs the question into my ear.

I bow my head, just slightly, just enough.

"And this?" He takes my right nipple between his thumb and finger, squeezes, at first lightly, then tightens his grip until I wince. He holds it, keeps the pressure on for a few seconds.

I'm arching against him, gasping, and he eventually releases me.

"Did I hurt you?"

I nod again, but make no attempt to move.

"Did you like it?"

Another bob of my head signals my pleasure.

"Mmm, sexy little sub. I love this top by the way, but I think it'd look much, much better folded up on the floor. Take it off, please."

I glance over my shoulder, catch his gaze again, but I don't hesitate. I lean forward and pull the crimson and black top over my head, fold it carefully then place it on the floor beside the settee. And I settle back against him.

"Take the skirt off too, please. And the thong this time."

The request was softly delivered, but I can feel as much as hear the thread of steel in there. He's relaxed, he's easy — we're here to have fun. But he's a Dom and I'm a submissive, or very nearly, and I'm expected to obey. I've never been naked in the dungeon before, nor in any of the public areas for that matter. It seems I will be tonight though. And again, I don't allow myself to hesitate. My skirt and thong are quickly deposited on the floor too, and again I lay back against Nicholas Hardisty, my body exposed, available, his to do what he wants with. I just hope it's going to be good.

"Tell me what you've done so far, on your voyages of discovery? I'm pretty sure no one's used your arse much before now, which does seem a waste. Am I right so far?"

Again, I signal my agreement with a slight dip of my chin. No need for the phone.

"What else? What other fairground attractions have you been on up to now?"

He's idly stroking my breasts again, gentle, soothing, arousing me. The electric current starts to zip around my body, that arcing triangle between both my nipples and my clit. Still, his words sting a bit and I tell him so.

Please don't make fun of me. I know that email was stupid.

He nuzzles my neck, and despite my little show of prickliness I tingle.

"Sorry, I didn't mean it like that. I'm just asking, and I do want to know. Tell me please."

I shrug, tilt my head to give him better access and decide to let it go.

Not much. Mostly it's just been spanking. And a ruler once, in the schoolroom upstairs. On my bum and then my hands. I hated that — my hands I mean. I use them a lot, but I could hardly move them for days. That Dom invited me to scene again, but I refused. Too scared. And then, a few weeks after that, I emailed you.

"I see. And how do you like to be fucked?"

I don't understand, what do you mean?

"From behind? Do you like to be on top? Underneath? Against a wall? Kneeling? Standing? I don't usually take requests, but I might with you. Just this once."

I don't know really. Limited experience, I suppose. From behind seems nice.

"Seems?"
His hand stills. Is this it? Is this the moment he decides I really am just too much bother? I start to panic, grab the phone again.

You promised. You promised me. You can't go back on it now.

He takes my chin in his hand and turns my head to make me meet his gaze. He looks puzzled. "Go back on what?"
I start to type again and he releases my chin to let me see the screen.

I'm twenty-three years old, and I know what I want. I want you. You promised we could go back up to our room and

He chuckles again before I can complete my sentence. "Well, aren't you eager? How nice. Okay, don't panic, a promise is a promise. And your inexperience is no use to you here. A liability in fact, someone could be clumsy, not realize and get carried away, really hurt you. Since you've asked so nicely, I will fuck you, and I'll do it very slowly, very gently, very thoroughly and very well. I'll stop short of fucking you till you faint—we really should work up to that more gradually—but you will see stars. And if you say please very prettily, I'll probably even agree to do it all over again, just to make sure you got the message. That suit you?"

I turn my head of my own volition this time, gape at him over my shoulder. *Christ, what an offer!* Then, a little belatedly perhaps, I try for some shred of decorum as I turn my attention back to the phone.

Yes, thank you, Sir. I think that should do very nicely.

"Well I'm glad we've got that sorted. Sounds like a plan. Now, before I start working on widening your experience in the fucking department, what would you like to do here? Any requests, anything you particularly fancy trying, or will you let me choose?"

I turn in his arms and point to his chest.

"Me then. Okay, something—intense—I think. A bit of edge but not too painful. Needs to be memorable though. And maybe a bit of a mind-fuck as a prelude to the body-fuck later. I know just the thing for you. Come on."

A mind-fuck? Not sure I like the sound of that. But still, when he stands, turns to me, his hand outstretched, I take it. Modesty abandoned, I get to my feet, naked, and follow him across the room. He leads me over to the dungeon-master, my usual protector. Frank is stationed behind a small desk at one end of the room. His strategic position means he can see everything that's happening, everywhere in his domain. Nothing goes on here that Frank doesn't know about and allow. He's huge and imposing — ex-Army I'm sure, and he rules the dungeon with a rod of iron. But I like him. Frank's always quite nice to us subs, especially the unattached ones like me. His job here, mainly, is to look out for us, to make sure no one takes anything too far, and that no one gets hurt. I appreciate Frank, his presence, his rules. But I don't usually parade around in front of him naked. He doesn't turn a hair though — not that he has much — just nods politely at us.

"Mr Hardisty, Freya, I trust you're both enjoying your evening."

Nicholas Hardisty smiles amiably, relaxed and casual, his arm loosely slung across my shoulders. "Yes, so far. And it promises to get even better. Could I trouble you for a blindfold please?"

"Of course. Anything else?"

"Yes, there will be later. Would you mind coming over to us in a few minutes please? For now just the blindfold though."

"Certainly." He turns to me then. "And may I ask, Freya, what arrangements have you agreed regarding safe words?"

I stand, waiting for Nicholas to answer for me. He offers nothing so I glance up at him. He just shrugs and gestures toward Frank with his head, indicating that I should speak for myself. I hold up my hands to show the huge guardian of public safety my new wristbands.

He nods once, this time directing the gesture at Mr Hardisty. "Very good. I assume red means 'stop' and the yellow means 'caution'?"

I nod, and smile confidently at him. I can do this. I can actually join in now and do this. Maybe I could have managed something along these lines before — it's hardly rocket science, just a couple of colored wristbands — but it's so incredibly difficult to explain even the simplest things, let alone negotiate, when the people around me don't understand signing. And even though I always have my phone or my iPad with me, it's in my bag, back in the cloakroom. No one here ever handed me their phone or a set of wristbands before.

Apparently satisfied that matters are under reasonable control, the huge man slips through a door behind him into a store room where lots of miscellaneous paraphernalia is kept. He returns a moment later with a thick felt blindfold, the sort that ties at the back. Nicholas turns to me immediately, places it over my eyes and ties it tightly around my head.

"Can you see anything?"

I shake my head, reaching out with my hands to feel where he is. He steps in front of me and I clutch the front of his shirt.

"As I said before, your eyes are very expressive, you tell me a lot with your eyes, about how you're feeling, how you're responding, and I'm taking a risk covering them. And what I have in mind for you tonight might feel strange, might surprise you, might frighten you a bit. It's meant to. But I won't hurt you. Do you trust me, Freya?"

I nod, but in reality, despite my wristbands, I'm pretty nervous. I feel totally cut off. He can't understand my signing, and without my sight I can't write, I can't communicate anything except with my wristbands. But now his hands are on my shoulders, stroking and soothing, his voice easing into my head, steadying and grounding me.

"Trust me, I won't let anything happen to you. And you can stop me at any time, you know that. Okay?"

I nod again. He takes my hand, and starts to lead me across the room. My footsteps falter as I follow him, terrified I'm going to trip or bump into something. I don't though, he smoothly negotiates me around the dungeon until I have absolutely no idea where I am or what equipment he has led me to. I'm disorientated and totally lost.

"Shuffle backwards, slowly." His soft instruction is murmured into my ear. I obey and feel something behind me, against my bare legs and back, some sort of apparatus, a solid structure.

"Raise your arms over your head."

Trusting still, I do as I'm told. And immediately wish I hadn't. He quickly secures my left wrist with a strap, then my right. It feels like leather and my arms are held above my head, my hands stretched wide apart. My last means of signaling suddenly withdrawn I start to tug, to struggle in earnest. He's there again, close, his breath against my ear.

"Be still, Freya, trust me."

But it's no good, I'm shaking my head wildly, scared, starting to lose it. He takes my face between his palms, holds my head still and places his mouth on mine.

The effect is instantaneous. His kiss, so unexpected, quiets and calms me, especially as my mouth instinctively opens under his and his tongue slides inside, exploring, tasting, claiming. One hand remaining on my face to hold me in position, he deepens the kiss, at the same time as his other hand slides down my body, across my breasts then farther, to tease the softly curling, neatly trimmed hair between my legs. He trails his hand through that, and between the slick folds. I arch, open my legs to let him in, and he accepts my invitation, plunging one finger deep inside me. Then, and only then, does he lift his head, breaking the kiss but remaining close—I can feel his breath on my face.

My body is moistening, his finger gently sliding in and out, my juices starting to flow in earnest now.

"I'm thinking you like this, little sub. Is that right?"

I nod then drop my head back as he continues to stroke me, adding a second finger to stretch me a little farther.

"Do you want me to stop?" His fingers go still, deep inside me but not moving now.

I shake my head, use my inner muscles to squeeze around him. Desperate, I want him to move, to stroke me, to give me the friction I suddenly require more than oxygen.

"Ah, that feels so good. And when you squeeze around me like that, whether it's my fingers inside you like now, or my cock later, that's another signal. That's you telling me, 'this is good, I like this, I want more of this'. Yeah? Does that make sense?"

I dip my head in understanding, but he hasn't finished yet.

"Can you make this sound?" He makes a clicking sound with his tongue, the sort of sound you might use for calling a dog over.

I nod, of course I can make that sound.

"Do it, let me hear it."

I click for him, and he drops another light kiss onto my mouth. "Not quite without vocal sounds then. That's your safe signal for this, while your hands are tied. If you need me to stop, or slow down, you click like that. I'll hear you, and I'll stop, check with you what you need, what you want to have happen. And if you want to stop, we will. So, are you okay still?"

I can manage a hearty whistle, but I never before considered clicking my tongue as a way of signaling. As I bow my head again, I admire his ingenuity. I'm not sure if he's making it up as he goes along or if he pre-planned all this, but it seems this inventive Dom has an answer for everything, a way of dealing with all my issues and problems. Angela was spot on in her recommendation. He was the right Dom to ask to train me. He could help me, he already has.

He takes my face between his palms. "I told you, upstairs, that I'd never lay a hand on you unless you had your safe words ready." His voice is low, sexy, sensual. And very firm as he continues. "You'll always be able to take back control whenever you want to. But submission, real submission, is when you choose not to, when you let your Dom have the power, and keep it, when you let your Dom do whatever he wants to with you, with your body, because that's the way you want it. Because it arouses you, excites you, fulfils you, because you want to please your Dom, and you trust him to always take care of you."

He stops, as though waiting for me to take that in, to assimilate this new thinking, re-align my beliefs and attitudes, my assumptions and pre-conceptions. Then, presumably when he thinks I've had enough time to get my head around it, he continues, "So, ready to play?"

I nod once more and wait. Nicholas steps away, and I'm lost without his close presence, bereft almost. I can hear his voice, low, nearby, and someone else answering. Frank? Then Nicholas is back, his hands on me once more, molding and squeezing my breasts. I let my head drop backwards, enjoying the sensation, even as he increases the pressure, lifting and squeezing, pressing my breasts together, running his thumbs across my nipples. My breathing hitches. I'm gasping, sighing—he must know how he's affecting me.

"Is this good? No clicking yet?" Sure enough, his voice is in my ear, checking.

I respond by arching my back, thrusting my breasts farther out, into his hands. He kisses my mouth again before dropping his head farther, taking my left nipple between his lips. He runs his tongue roughly around it before sucking, hard. He presses the engorged bud against the roof of his mouth and the exquisite pressure is beyond anything I have ever felt. The pleasure is almost too much, too intense. I'm panting, rigid as he continues to work my distended tip mercilessly.

Then when I'm sure I must need to click, I can't bear any more, he lets me go. Only to latch his mouth around my right nipple and repeat the performance. This time though his fingers are rolling my already erect left nipple, keeping the pressure on, building the sensation there as he brings the right tip up to the same heightened level of intense sensitivity. Moisture is pooling between my legs, my wetness increasing with every tug on my buds. My legs are free to move, and I try vainly to squeeze them harder together, somehow, trying to create the friction there, to sooth the throbbing in my clit.

Nicholas realizes what I'm about and puts a stop to it. "Oh no, little sub. You haven't earned that yet. Your clit can wait its turn. Until I'm good and ready." He releases my sore tip and crouches at my feet, quickly securing my ankles so that my legs are spread wide.

Then he stands, and although I can't see him and he's no longer touching me, I can feel his presence, his eyes all over me, admiring me, admiring his handiwork.

"Have you worked out where you are?"

I think I might be on the St. Andrew's Cross, but I'm not certain. I shake my head slowly.

"Think. Think harder. You do know, don't you? And you know what you've seen happening here, to other subs. Don't you, Miss Stone?"

I start to shake my head again, but he takes my face in his hands, holds me still. "Now, Freya, you know how things can get if you're not entirely honest with me. No games, no evading. Now, I'll ask you again. Do you know where you are?"

I nod.

His closeness is comforting, reassuring, despite the veiled threat of a moment ago. "The St Andrew's Cross, right?" His voice is low and sexy, and right by my ear.

I nod again.

"And you have your back to the wall, so you can be sure, this time at least, I don't intend to whip you. At least, not a punishment whipping. This is all about arousal, sweetheart. And it starts here, with these."

He takes both my nipples between his thumbs and forefingers, rolling at first but quickly increasing the pressure, squeezing and pulling until I'm gasping under the onslaught of pain. "I'm going to do this until you click. I want to know how much you can take. When it becomes unbearable, let me know. Okay?"

I grind my teeth, stiffen against the straps holding me in place as he relentlessly twists, squeezes and pulls my nipples. And after a few seconds he has what he wants. I click my tongue, and he stops increasing the torment. He doesn't release me though, just holds me in that place between intense pain and—what— exquisite pleasure dancing just out of reach. Confused, maybe just a little frightened, I chew my bottom lip as I'm held there, helpless in his hands, waiting to feel whatever comes next.

I almost sigh with relief as he lets go of my nipples, only to jerk back to full, alert awareness as something bites down hard, first on my left nipple then on the right. It's not sharp, but it's tight and mean and the grip is vicious. A weight is tugging at me, dragging my nipples downwards. I try to move, but the pressure increases, the heavy object swinging, pulling, tormenting me. It's awful, frankly awful. I can't bear it.

"Don't struggle, just let your nipples adjust. It feels strange now, but you can do this." His voice is gentle, so are his hands as he holds and shapes my breasts, taking the weights suspended from them to allow me a brief respite before allowing them to fall free again. He repeats the action, each time the shock is a little less, the pain just slightly more bearable.

I know he's clamped my nipples, I've watched this sort of scene often enough. But I've never envied the subs playing, this is not what I would have chosen as my initiation into the delights of the dungeon.

I shiver as the tip of Nicholas' tongue lightly flicks the very tip of my left nipple, the small part protruding beyond the vicious clamp. The blood supply trapped there makes me super-sensitive and the electric tingle shoots straight to my clit. He repeats the action, this time on my right nipple, and I jerk involuntarily. The sensation is truly exquisite, I'm able to experience the pleasure beyond the pain. I'm beginning to fully understand the point of this. Now I know for myself what those other submissives I've watched were feeling. But this is not second hand pleasure, vicarious fun, the joy of voyeurism. I'm sure I'll never tire of watching others, I do love that, but I always wanted to participate too. I felt excluded, but no more.

My Dom is a Master, he knows exactly what he's doing. The blindfold concentrates my senses. No sight, but all my other faculties are sharply honed. Touch, hearing — all sensation centered on my breasts, my nipples and that crackling link to my inner core.

He's made no move to touch me other than at my breasts. But I know that even the slightest attention to my clit at this point would send me into orbit. And I need that. I need to tell him, I need him to help me. I'm thrashing around on the cross, as far as I'm able, held securely in place by the straps at my wrists and ankles. Nicholas is not touching me now, my own movements are causing the weights suspended from the nipple clamps to swing and pull on me, each movement increasing my torment. Then he's back, the backs of his knuckles now trailing from my throat, down between my breasts to my navel. And there he stops. I'm grinding my teeth in frustration now, and he knows it. He damned well knows everything that's going on in my aroused, tingling body and he's playing me like a violin.

"I have more planned for you, but you're not much use to me like this. Too wound up, too unstable, too volatile. So I'm going to let you come, just once, quick and hard to release the pressure. Then we start again, and next time you'll control yourself better. Won't you, little sub?" His tone is cool and clipped, with maybe a hint of displeasure there.

I don't want him angry, disappointed in me. But I can't bear this, I need to climax so much. I'll promise anything. I bob my head quickly to signal what I want, what I need so desperately, the only means of communication left to me.

And he's quick to respond. He uses both hands, parts my labia quickly and efficiently and slides his fingers between to circle my pussy swiftly before plunging two fingers deep inside me. I jerk, thrust my hips out, begging silently for more. And he obliges, gives me more. His thumb is on my clit, he rubs once, twice, and on the third stroke I detonate. I throw my head back, my mouth open in a silent scream of utter delight and satisfaction as I experience the most powerful, most explosive, most shattering orgasm I have ever had. Up to now my best orgasms have, in fairness, been solo efforts, but this is everything I've ever managed to achieve for myself and much more. This climax is like everything I've felt before, now rolled up into one explosive burst of energy pulsing through me. It hits me in seconds, and it's over almost as quickly as it began. Nicholas wastes no time, forcing my response, pushing me hard over the edge and catching me quickly on the other side.

"That's good, but enough for now. Now, you concentrate on what I'm doing to you, on what I'm saying to you, and you control yourself. You won't come again until I give you permission to. Is that clear, girl?"

I sag against my restraints and he immediately jerks me back to the here and now by tugging hard on both weights. "Pay attention. And answer me. Now."

Startled, unnerved by his sudden change in mood, I shrink away from him.

"Don't cower." He doesn't take kindly to my response. "You know better than that. Remember, you're in control here. You can always click if you want me to stop. Now, answer my question—do you understand your instructions? You are not to come again without my permission. Is. That. Clear?"

I concentrate on breathing deeply, evenly, as I nod my response. Yes, matters are perfectly clear to me. I'm suspended, naked, from a St. Andrew's Cross, my nipples brutally clamped. I've just been treated to the best orgasm ever which has suddenly transformed into some sort of crime I don't understand, but if I do it again I'll be punished. He has something else planned for me, something more, I don't know what that is, but it appears that if I have the temerity to like it too much and come again, he'll punish me for that. I'm scared, confused, constantly off balance and apprehensive about what comes next.

And Nicholas Hardisty knows all of this. He's inside my head. Again. This, no doubt, is what he meant by a mind-fuck.

His voice is low as he murmurs into my ear, "Welcome to submission, little Freya. Is it all you hoped for?"

Chapter Four

Bewildered, I shake my head. Is that the right answer? I have no idea what to do, how to respond. Thankfully, Nicholas Hardisty lets it go at that, kindly not pressing me. In fairness, the most I could possibly communicate to him is my all-stop signal, and neither of us wants that. Yet.

He steps away. Or I think he does. I can't hear him breathing close by me, and my hearing is very acute. Most of the time. I wait, conscious that he's left me here, on display, totally helpless. And until he comes back there's absolutely nothing I can do to change anything. The sense of freedom, of liberation, is extreme. Heady. Exhilarating. This is the buzz of submission for me, the handing over control, letting someone else hold the responsibility while I fly. And somehow, if he chooses to, I know Nicholas Hardisty can make me soar.

"You look happy, little sub. Something amusing you?" His low, sexy voice is in my ear, murmuring.

He's close by, and I never heard him approaching. I gasp as he nudges the weights suspended from my nipples, causing a tingle of pleasure/pain to crackle through me, from my tortured breasts to my groin, a sizzling triangle of perfect agony. I'm groaning inside, though he hears nothing.

"Are you liking this, little sub? Do you want more or shall we move on to the next phase?" Despite my lack of sounds he knows. He sees something which gives him the clues he needs.

I'm wondering how to tell him I want to move on when, with no warning or preamble, he slides two long fingers swiftly into me, filling my pussy with his brisk, skilled presence. A third quickly joins the first two, and I'm delightfully stretched, clinging around him, the friction as he twists his hand to caress my inner walls gloriously satisfying.

"Squeeze me, once if you want to stay with this a bit longer, and twice if you want to try out what's coming next."

I change my mind, and squeeze once. He chuckles, treats me to a swift finger fuck, just two or three plunges before pulling his fingers out. "Greedy little sub, I told you not to even think about coming again until I give you permission. And you *are* thinking about it, aren't you?"

Lost, confused, I shake my head quickly, the gesture more one of bewilderment than denial.

"Was that a 'no'? Are you denying it, little sub? Because here tells a different story." His fingers slide back into me, their entry easy, slick with my wetness.

The juicy, wet sound of his fingers working me is unmistakable evidence of my intense arousal. He withdraws his hand and lifts it to cup my chin. My own juices are now spread across my face, the wetness cooling my cheek in the warm room. He holds me still and brushes his lips over mine.

"So scared, so confused. Do you still trust me, sexy, randy little sub?"

I gulp, chew my bottom lip—a nervous habit of mine, one he's no doubt noting—and I nod. Despite it all, despite how nervous he makes me feel, how much he intimidates me, I do trust Nicholas Hardisty.

"Good. Let's get on with it then." His brisk, business-like tone belies the sensuous trail of his fingertips from my chin along my shoulder and down the outside curve of my right breast.

Carefully not disturbing the clamps, he feathers his thumbs, I think it's his thumbs, across the small portion of each nipple not tightly clasped between the grips. I tingle once more. The tortured peaks are rock hard, the blood trapped there making them ultra-sensitized to even the slightest touch. His tongue replaces his thumbs, the soft flick across the distended little buds achingly, unbearably tender.

He repeats the caress, both nipples at once this time. I gasp, jerk back, causing the weights to swing and the clamps to bite me even harder. Not his tongue then. And not his fingers either, too soft. Again, that feather-light almost touch, almost not. I'm desperately trying to imagine what he's using, what he's touching me with. It doesn't hurt, and it's too light, too delicate, to be truly arousing. Isn't it?

He draws that light 'something' across both my nipples once more. Slowly. It's fluid, muted, incredibly intense. And so very arousing. I remember his instruction not to come, and I wonder how long I'll be able to hold out. A while. Maybe, as long as he doesn't…

I gasp as he turns his attention—and his feather-like implement—to my clit. *Oh, God, not good. So good.* I can't bear this, I have to come. I need to come. Now.

I'm shaking, almost sobbing under the cruel duress of fighting my out-of-control arousal. Of trying desperately to tamp it down. I need the release, and it's coming soon—I know it. I can't fight it for much longer, but I'm too scared of his reaction if I disobey him. I can't let him down, can't disappoint him. But I need…

"Are you thinking about coming without permission, greedy, disobedient little sub?"

His low voice is like a splash of cold water, reminding me who's Master here. I shake my head violently, grinding my teeth as I squeeze down hard on my inner emptiness, clenching everything at my core in a last, desperate attempt to obey him.

And merciful at last, he decides to help me out. I flinch as a sharp flicker of almost-pain shoots across the front of my right thigh. He waits a moment before the next stroke, which connects with my left thigh, just under that little hollow where my leg meets my groin. It's some sort of a lash, like a whip but not quite. It falls again, this time across my stomach, and a little harder now. It *is* pain. Not the searing pain of the paddle across my bottom earlier in the evening, but definitely uncomfortable. And getting worse. He adds a little more bite with each stroke, each lash carefully placed and accurately judged to lay exactly the right sensation on my body. I'm quivering, jerking each time he flogs me. He moves to my breasts—already throbbing and unbearably tender, still cruelly gripped in the nipple clamps—and delivers several lashes to the undersides before moving to the upper curves. He's ramping up the pressure now, each stroke stinging a whisker more than the last, and they're coming at me thick and fast. The pressure builds as he lays the flogger across my breasts, my stomach, my abdomen, and back to that vulnerable, sensitive, undefended space between my legs. And he gentles his touch again. Just when I expected, anticipated the cruel sting of the lash to strike me where it would hurt the most, he turns it into the most delicate caress.

"Come now, little sub."

His voice is soft, a command, but murmured so quietly I have to strain to hear him. But it's enough, and as he draws the soft strand once more across my clit, I explode. Or implode. Whatever, it just about knocks me senseless as the powerful punch of orgasm whips through me. I would have hit the floor but for the restraints holding me in place. He continues to stroke my clit, caressing me. He's skillfully drawing out the moment, stretching it impossibly. I now know why he forced me to wait. He knew the impact of anticipation, he appreciated how much better this would be for letting it build. I'm shaking with the sheer, intense force of the sensations rocking my body, shuddering under this onslaught which seems to be endless. Deliciously, mind-blowingly, superbly endless.

And even when the shudders and pulsing energy start to subside, he starts them up again by slipping his expert fingers into me once more. He twists his hand, stretching and caressing me to bring me back up to melting point again, just to hold me there for a few moments before angling his fingers to hit that spot and send me hurtling back into orbit. He's relentless, but generous too. Both demanding and giving, playing me expertly. I'm gasping for breath, dragging oxygen in when I can remember to, but mostly just caught up in existing in this tiny world which now comes down to my pussy, my clit and his beautiful fingers doing their work. The pain in my breasts, the sting of the lash, every other sensation is driven from me by the intensity of what's happening at this moment, in this moment. There's nothing else.

It seems an eternity before my body is even remotely mine again, before the swirling, commanding grip of orgasm gives way to the sweet aftershocks — the more gentle, intimate pulsing of grateful surrender. I start to become aware of my surroundings once more, and of the pain elsewhere in my body. I want, need, to be released from this cross, the clamps removed, but I can't ask him.

I don't need to, he knows.

"I have you, you're safe. I'm going to take the blindfold off first…"

I blink as the light, dimmed though it is, hits my eyes. He cups my chin, smiling at me, and I smile back. He's so beautiful, so damned beautiful. He kisses my mouth, sliding his tongue quickly past my lips to caress and explore. I feel…precious, valued, cared for. He lifts his head, regards me ruefully as he drops his hand to cup my left breast.

"It'll hurt when I take these off, but I'll help you with that. On a count of three, first the left, then the right. Are you ready?"

I nod, trusting him.

"One. Two. Three…"

On the third count I rear back. Searing pain grips me momentarily when he releases the clamp biting into my left nipple, and the blood flow rushes into the hard, distended bud. Then, just as suddenly, the pain's gone. The tender tip is once more held, pressed, sucked hard as he drops his head and takes it between his lips, using his tongue to press my tortured, delicate nipple against the roof of his mouth. Once in control he releases the pressure slowly, allowing me time to adjust. *God, where did he learn tricks like this?* Long moments pass, and I'm still again, quiet, relaxing as he helps me back.

"Now the right one, okay? One. Two. Three." He repeats his clever trick, squeezing my nipple hard in his mouth, only relaxing the pressure little by little to restore the blood flow in easy stages.

At last, I'm there, and he lifts his head, one eyebrow raised in query. I nod my confirmation, I *am* well. Bending, he retrieves the nipple clamps and weights from the floor where he tossed them and hands them to Frank who has appeared behind him. Frank accepts them and the discarded blindfold. He's already holding a brown suede flogger, which I assume was Nicholas' chosen instrument, now done with. Frank nods and winks at me, then turns on his heel to leave us to it.

A sudden thought hits me—was Frank there the whole time? Did he witness my unraveling at close quarters? Maybe it shouldn't matter, but I find it does. The dungeon is no place for those who value their privacy, and I daresay I must be something of an exhibitionist, but even so...

The amazing Nicholas Hardisty telepathy is on full beam again as my Master for the evening shakes his head, smiling gently at me. "He was around, keeping an eye on you. But he only just came over when I signaled him to. It was just us, Freya." He kisses me again, just a swift brush of his lips across mine before he crouches to unbuckle the straps at my ankles.

My legs free, he stands and reaches for the wrist restraints, this time using just one hand as he circles my waist with his other arm. Sure enough, as the second strap gives way, I collapse into his arms, my legs just jelly under me. He scoops me up, effortlessly, and strides the few feet to a spot where beanbags and huge cushions are strewn across the floor. Sinking onto a bean bag with me still in his arms, Nicholas Hardisty leans back, relaxes. I lift my arms, link my fingers behind his neck and lay my cheek against his chest. And for the first time I realize he is naked from the waist up. At some point in our scene he has taken off his shirt—I suppose whipping me must have been strenuous work—and now I'm held cradled against that gorgeous expanse of chiseled, sculpted male perfection.

I wince slightly as he trails his palm down my back and across my bum, the legacy of the paddle still in evidence but somehow pleasantly so by now. He feels my slight shiver of pain and repeats his caress, lingering on my most sore bits, but it's wonderfully intimate that he can do this, that he knows where to touch me. I tighten my hold around his neck as he nuzzles my shoulder, lightly kissing and alternating with little nips. I turn into him, my breasts still tender, but again, a pleasant sensation now as I press them against the hard, unyielding planes of his body. I'd stay here forever if I could, if we could, if he would.

"God, I need to fuck you, Freya. Is that still okay with you?" His tone is low, seductive. And determined.

And suddenly, there's only one place I want to be. Room nine. I nod. Hard. And he chuckles, standing and placing me on my feet. "Upstairs then. Now."

At first I think he means me to make my own way and wait dutifully for him in room nine, the perfect submissive, especially as he steps away from me. And even though I don't relish the prospect of being forced to walk naked and alone through the building, I'm quite prepared to do that, I know how these things work, what the Dom/sub protocol is. But I quickly realize that's not what he has in mind at all. He retrieves his shirt from the woodwork of the cross where he must have draped it at some point earlier, then he turns back to me. He holds it out by the shoulders for me to slip my arms through. He then closes the buttons, leaving me decent, and patently marked out as his.

He holds out his hand, and I lace my fingers through his as we start to stroll back across the room. He detours to our original perch on the settee in the middle of the dungeon. Another couple are now ensconced there—a huge Dom is lounging casually with an equally huge male sub kneeling at his feet, head bowed as the Master idly strokes his naked shoulders with a cruel looking leather tawse. I know a lot of the other subs, but I don't recognize him. I gulp at the sight of the instrument his Master apparently intends to use, thick and heavy and extremely vicious.

Nicholas Hardisty nods companionably to the other Dom as he bends to pick up my clothes, still neatly folded beside the settee. He totally ignores the sub, whose eyes never lift from his knees, and we move on. He gestures for me to precede him through the door to the stairs, another surprise because regardless of gender and 'outside' courtesy norms, Doms do not defer to subs here. Whatever, I do as he's indicated I should, and lead the way up the stairs. At the top he takes my hand again, and I note he is still carrying my clothes too as we make our way along the corridor toward the stairs leading to the upstairs rooms.

As we stroll in silence along the corridor, Nicholas pulls his phone from his pocket, hits a few quick keystrokes then speaks into it to order coffee to be brought to room nine. Maybe he thinks I'm worn out after all his — and my — exertions and need the caffeine hit. And maybe he's right. He turns to me, asks if I'm hungry. I shake my head, no point pushing my luck, and he regards me doubtfully for a few moments. "You will be," his only comment before he proceeds to ask for a selection of snacks too. A picnic then? I'm to be fucked, then fed — or maybe the other way around...

He ends the call and hands the phone to me. "In case you get chatty, Miss Stone." He grins.

His grin is infectious, beautiful, and I can't help smiling back. I should be terrified, or at least respectfully nervous given that my sexual horizons are about to be significantly expanded, but I feel I'm walking on air. There's nothing soft or sentimental about Nicholas Hardisty. I know he's a hard, stern Dom — my bottom can testify to that — but he's being incredibly nice to me just now. Just when I need it.

We reach the door to 'our' room and he stops, turns, leans his back on it. He pulls me to him, his hands on my hips, catches my gaze. "Point of no return, Miss Stone. If you've had enough for this evening, you can say so, just wave your red wristband at me. Or the yellow if you're not sure..."

My response is to link my hands behind his neck again and reach up to kiss him. And he lets me, another unusual response for a Dom, especially with a new or temporary sub. Maybe he appreciates my need to use other signals as I have no spoken words, or maybe he's off duty now...? Somehow, though, I doubt that.

He smiles and reaches for the door handle at his back, and in the next moment we're inside and he closes it behind us. There's no lock, the staff here insist on being able to enter any room, and the small but discreet CCTV camera mounted in a corner above the door guarantees we'll never be totally alone—Frank and co. know their responsibilities. But I dismiss that, for now, it's just him and me.

Nicholas Hardisty advances toward me, and instinctively I back up, as he must have known I would. In moments the bed is behind my knees, and with a gentle shove Nicholas tumbles me onto it. He follows me down, his hands around my wrists as he raises them above my head to gently hold them against the pillow. He takes the phone from between my fingers and places it carefully beside me, still within reach of my left hand. I realize I haven't used it yet, not since we left the dungeon. Not so chatty after all, when it comes right down to it.

But I do have one question, one very important question. I strain against him, and he immediately releases my left hand. I reach for the phone and quickly type in my question.

Am I allowed to come?

He looks at the screen and smiles down at me. "Oh yes, Miss Stone. In fact, it's compulsory. A minimum of three times or it doesn't really count."

I look at him in astonishment—I'd settle for just once, anything really. He grins—playful and teasing suddenly, a sharp contrast to the stern Dom I had to contend with the first time I was in this room. "You seem surprised, Miss Stone. Not enough for you? Do you think we should be aiming higher? Four? Five? Even more?"

Confused, but secretly delighted at the way this evening is turning out, I drop the phone as he leans in to kiss me, only to scramble for it again as something else occurs to me. With a resigned expression he halts, and passes it to me. I smile my thanks, and type in another question.

Am I allowed to touch you?

Now this one throws him. He doesn't answer immediately, obviously considering. Then he takes my chin, holds my face up so I can't drop my gaze from his. "You know that's not the usual way of it, don't you, Freya? The Dom fucks, the sub takes it. That's how I like it."

I start to nod my acceptance, silly question really, as he pushes up off the bed to stand over me. He looks down at me sternly, and for an awful moment I'm sure I've blown it. I've clearly irritated him with my naïve, vanilla-like ways, and now he's decided I'm not worth the bother after all.

But then, with that gorgeous, sexy smile back on his face, he unsnaps his jeans and drops the zip. He starts to peel the jeans off, pulling them down over his hips and lifting each knee in turn to pull them past his ankles and step out of them. For a moment he's there in front of me, just wearing shiny, black, silky boxer shorts, his erection tenting proudly, just inches from my face. I watch, mesmerized, as he pulls his shorts down too and steps out of them. In moments he's standing before me in all his erect male glory.

I've seen plenty of cocks before, this place is full of them—as often as not on display. Especially the male submissives, but the Doms aren't exactly shy either, in a more functional way. But Nicholas Hardisty is something else entirely. With his clothes on he was superb, naked he's beyond wonderful, beyond anything I ever imagined. His chest I already explored at close quarters, but I'll never get tired of admiring all those sculpted planes and sharp angles. His pectorals are clearly defined, his chest sprinkled with a dusting of dark brown hair which gets thicker as it snakes down across his flat stomach—the six pack clearly defined—to pool at his groin. His pubic hair is dark brown too, framing that beautiful cock. I know it's rude, and I know it shows my total lack of any real and meaningful experience, but I'm staring, transfixed. If it were actually possible to roll my eyes out on stalks, I'd be doing just that at this moment. His low tone is amused as he breaks into my trance-like state.

"I know you're curious, and from what you say you've not had that many opportunities to explore. And I promised to make it good for you. Really good. So yeah, just this once, you can touch if you want to."

I gape up at him, and he smiles back at me. "I'm all yours, sweetheart. I don't usually do this so don't waste your opportunity."

I run my tongue across my lower lip, realizing my mouth is dry, and I wonder what the hell to do next. Could I? Should I? Can I just reach out and…?

"If it's my cock you're most interested in, just start by stroking it with your fingertips. Along the shaft and around the head. Feel the texture. Explore. If you run your thumb around the top it'll get wet, like you do." He hesitates for a moment, then, "Taste it, if you want."

Christ, do I want! I reach out with both hands and tentatively run my fingers along the length of his shaft. It's incredibly smooth and silky, but hard to the touch, utterly solid. I wrap my fingers around it and find I can't quite close my hand around the thickness. I know without any doubt that this will fit inside me, at least that's the theory, but still—it seems a stretch. For a moment my head is filled with the crazy and irrelevant image of a tiny pair of new tights coming out of their packet, and the extent to which they then stretch to accommodate my legs. My pussy must be like that. Well, it's to be hoped so.

I run my fingers up the shaft and across the shiny, dark-pink colored head. He hisses, and I glance up sharply, afraid I've done it wrong. Worse still, hurt him. Although why I should feel concerned at that after all he's done to me this evening, I really can't fathom. His smile is gentle and reassuring though, and his hand in my hair tells me I'm doing fine.

"That feels good, little Freya. Now, cup my balls with one hand and stroke the shaft with the other."

I do as I'm told, and I'm rewarded by a definite twitching under my hands, and more soft hissing. "Mmm, you're a fast learner, Miss Stone. Now, squeeze a little harder and speed up. You can squeeze my balls too, but please, not too hard…"

I turn my attention totally to the huge penis in my hand, still not quite believing I'm doing this, that he's allowing me such freedom with his body. When I asked to touch him I didn't really expect him to agree, and certainly not to give me such free rein. He said I could taste him too so I slip off the bed to kneel on the floor in front of him, and of course he knows what's coming. I lean forward, and run the tip of my tongue around the head of his cock, his hand suddenly fists in my hair. I take that as a signal this is okay—he'd be easily able to pull my head away from him if it wasn't, and I do it again, lapping delicately. The fluid tastes salty, and I lick my lips in appreciation. Without stopping to consider, I open my mouth wide and take the entire head inside, rolling my tongue around it as I continue to slide my hand up and down the shaft. Nicholas reacts instantly, leaning into me, his other hand also plowing through my hair as he holds my head steady. But he doesn't push, doesn't start to thrust or force me to take him deeper.

It's me who does that. I'm the one opening my mouth even wider, swallowing hard to clear the salty juices and maintain my airway as I lean in to draw more of the shaft into my mouth. The head of his cock is against the back of my throat and I start to gag. He pulls back slightly, but I grasp him more firmly, raise my eyes to his in silent appeal that he let me finish. Or at least let me try. He nods, and his fingers firm in my hair as I continue to explore with my mouth, loving the tastes and textures, the sense of being in control of a dangerous, powerful animal. I'm loving that I can make him hiss and shudder, and soon learn how to get those responses. Which little flick of my tongue, squeeze of my lips, scrape of my teeth will make him jerk in my mouth and cause those delicious juices to flow even faster. I'm vaguely aware of my own arousal building too, and I know that moisture is gathering beneath me. When he does finally get to touch me—and I'm sure it won't be much longer before the almighty Dom takes back the reins—he'll be in no doubt as to my readiness to be thoroughly fucked.

"I'm going to come in your mouth, little Freya. You'll swallow it, all of it." The commanding timbre is back, that tone that demands obedience.

I *will* be swallowing his semen, like it or not. And I know who's really in control here, has been all along. Still, it's been a wonderfully pleasant illusion. And I will most certainly be swallowing anything that he ejaculates into my mouth. Every drop.

Moments later, that's put to the test. The hot, salty semen spurts out, filling my mouth and throat, the stream seemingly endless. His grip has tightened in my hair, and I'm not sure I could disengage even if I wanted to, but he pulls back slightly to give me room, breathing space. I swallow frantically, clear my throat only to have it filled again as he continues to ejaculate. I stiffen, stunned a little at the sheer quantity of it, but I'm not giving in. This is mine. I did this. I caused this. I'm having all of it.

At last, the flow diminishes, then stops, and his fingers loosen in my hair. I raise my eyes again and meet his. The slate gray is almost gone, his pupils dilated in passion, and with an inner glow of smug satisfaction I know I caused that too. I gave Nicholas Hardisty a blow-job, for Christ's sake. Me, little Freya Stone. And he liked it, obviously.

"Well, Miss Stone, aren't you full of surprises? That was unexpected. Very welcome though." He pulls back, withdrawing from my mouth, stopping for a moment to gaze down at me, still kneeling at his feet. He crouches, cups my chin. "And you did yourself a favor too, your little antics have taken the edge off for me so now I can give you a lot more attention. A whole lot more. Would you like that, Freya?"

I nod, and he smiles at me before standing up again. He turns to stroll gloriously naked and unembarrassed across the room. There's a small en suite shower and loo in the corner of the room and he slips inside, to re-emerge a moment later with a box of tissues. Pulling one out, he crouches in front of me once more to wipe my face, my mouth. Then he kisses me, just briefly, before leaning back to lick his lips. I know he tastes himself on me, and if his sexy smile is any indication, he's rather pleased with the flavor of my lips just now.

"You're over-dressed, Miss Stone. Lose the shirt." His casual tone is in contrast to the intensity of his gaze, now raking me.

He looks…hungry, and I lose no time in slipping the buttons of the shirt he lent to me and sliding it off my shoulders. He smiles again, then, moving suddenly, he scoops me up off the floor and dumps me on the bed, following me down in a tangle of limbs and lust. His erection has hardly diminished at all following my ministrations—he's clearly ready to go again immediately. I suspect I am too, but can't quite manage to quell a little flutter of nerves. I find myself underneath Nicholas Hardisty's long, lean, strong body, with his right knee between my legs. He's supporting his weight on his elbows so not crushing me, not quite, but I'm effectively pinned in place. He dips his head to nuzzle my neck as he encircles my wrists with his hands. His voice is low, murmuring in my ear.

"I usually like to tie my subs up at this point, but I think perhaps not with you, not this time. Nice, hands-free fucking, Miss Stone. You up for that?"

He lifts his head to catch my gaze, and I know if I want to back out, now's probably the only chance I'll get. From here on in he's in control and unless I say the word—or more accurately wave the wristband—I'm accepting, consenting, to whatever happens next. My hands stay still, and I smile, my eyes clear as I hold his gaze, steady and sure. With a curt nod, he rolls to my side, propping himself up on one elbow to trail his gaze along my body, appraising, admiring maybe…

"Looking good, Miss Stone. God, you really are one sexy little sub aren't you? How come I never spotted you before, even if you did hide in the corner...? How come no one spotted you? You should have been very well fucked indeed, lots of times, well before now."

Admiring then, definitely. Thank goodness. He glances back into my face, his expression one of wry humor. "Still, better late than never, don't you think?"

Before I can think of anything at all, he's trailing his fingers down my body, lightly teasing my left nipple with the back of his hand. I wince, ever so slightly.

"Still tender?"

I nod, shrug, and he smiles at me. "Don't worry, little Freya, no more rough stuff now. This is going to feel good, really good. If I hurt you, even a little, you let me know. Yes?"

I nod once more, beginning to feel a lot like one of those little dogs you sometimes see on the rear parcel shelf of an old Ford Cortina. Then I gasp as Nicholas' mouth follows the trail blazed by his fingers. He gently takes my abused nipple in his mouth, lightly flicks it with the tip of his tongue while I arch under him, offering him more. All previous ill-treatment forgotten, this feels just wonderful, fabulous, absolutely heavenly.

He moves his attention to my right nipple, and I wriggle under him, my fists clutching at the pillow on either side of my head as he continues to suckle, so light, so delicate, all his previous intense forcefulness carefully and completely leashed now as he nibbles softly. He's in no hurry—takes his time before nudging lower, dropping feather light kisses across my stomach before he curls his tongue into my belly button. I buck, it tickles, and he drops an arm across me to hold me still as he continues to play. At last he heads south still farther, combing his fingertips through my soft pubic hair before glancing back up at me.

"Open, please." His words are low, his voice now a mere seductive whisper.

I obey immediately, eagerly. He slides his fingers between my legs, parting the sleek, sensitive folds there, his eyes still holding mine as he gauges my reaction. And my reaction is, I suspect, quite unambiguous. And totally uninhibited. I buck and thrust under his hand, desperately seeking the friction, the pressure, the penetration I desire more than air. He cruelly avoids my clit—despite my frantic efforts to thrust that greedy, swollen little nub at him—preferring to part my labia and circle my entrance slowly. I'm tensing, all my attention focused on those three or four square inches of sensitive, aroused flesh under his skilled fingers. In this moment that's all there is to me, an intense core of burning need, waiting, pleading silently for him to, to…

Yes! I almost come off the bed as he at last slides two fingers inside me, thrusting hard, adjusting the angle to cause maximum devastation to my already shattered senses. My orgasm starts to bubble immediately, the familiar tightening low down in my stomach as my body prepares for another climax. Momentarily I recall the awful pressure of earlier in the evening when he forbade me to come, and even though he told me that it's okay now, that I can and should come as often as I like, I still look to him for confirmation. And get it in the form of his knowing smile and sexy wink. It's enough, and my orgasm bursts from me like a volcanic eruption, some unstoppable force of nature unleashed. I'm rocked by it, beyond conscious thought, beyond remembering my own name.

He doesn't stop there. The instant I start to quieten again, he starts on my clit at last, rubbing it with his thumb to prolong my release, or re-start it, who knows? All I know is the fabulous pulsing, shuddering, earth-rocking storm is flying at me from all sides now and I think I may be in orbit. I'm spinning, out of control, dizzy, clutching wildly at the pillow for some semblance of solid anchor to see me through this storm of sensation. My body clenches and spasms helplessly, my legs spread wide to offer him greater access, pleading with him to take it, use it, use me.

And at last, I am through, and tumbling down to earth again on the other side. My entire body feels like jelly, boneless, and my breath is hitching. I suspect I may have suffered some form of oxygen deprivation damage — it seems so long since I last dragged in a decent breath. My eyes are closed as I slowly come back into the here and now, re-acquaint myself with the real world, my surroundings — the beautiful man now holding me against his chest as the last of the tremors escape my body. He tangles his fingers in my hair, lightly stroking it until I calm again, until my eyes are focused and I seem, at least outwardly, in control. Then he starts again.

"That was excellent, Miss Stone. Very nice indeed. I think we'll be having another of those, don't you?"

Another? Not likely. Not in this lifetime...

Maybe if I could have gotten some words across to him I might have expressed my serious doubt that another such orgasm could ever possibly exist again anywhere in the known universe. But I can't, so instead I watch helplessly while he slides off the bed to kneel on the floor, pulling me to lie across the bed, my bum near the edge closest to him. My feet are dangling, just touching the floor, but he takes each of my ankles and places them on the edge of the bed, my knees bent. Then, slowly, deliberately, he pushes my knees apart, wide apart, opening me to his gaze. Despite everything he's done to me already this evening, this is the first time he's examined me so closely, so intimately, and I'm unaccountably embarrassed. Even so, and with some effort, I make no attempt to close my legs or hide from him. I remain still, let him look, and hope he likes what he sees.

I needn't have worried. "So pretty, Miss Stone. And red as a cherry. You're really very eager, aren't you?"

I'm not sure if I should be answering that, but on this occasion he seems not to intend to press me on it, preferring to devote his attention to placing his thumbs on either side of my labia and pulling them apart, gently opening me. He leans forward, blows onto my sensitive, engorged flesh, and I shiver, the gesture so intimate. He slides his thumbs up, toward my clitoris then gently pulls back the delicate folds surrounding it, causing my clit to stand even prouder, even needier, desperate to be touched. Licked. Sucked.

He does all three, in that order. And I put up a valiant fight, enduring his sensual onslaught for all of seven or eight seconds before orgasm takes me once more. It's gentler this time, less intense, less the earth-scorching firestorm and more the howling gale that goes on all night, rattling windows and toppling roof slates. He plays me like a maestro, holding me at or around the point of orgasm for what seems like eons, frequently tipping me over the edge, just to catch me on the other side and toss me back up again. He knows exactly what he's doing, how he's affecting me, how my body's responding, and each time I think he's finished, that maybe I'm done now, he starts me up again. I'm not writhing and thrusting under him, rather I'm lying still in his hands, like a baby bird, shivering and helpless and hoping to simply survive.

And at last, at long, long last, he decides I've had enough. He delivers several last hard laps around my clit then sinks his tongue deep into my pussy, wringing one last lingering shudder of bone-deep satisfaction from me before he slowly lowers my legs, easing me back onto the length of the bed and moving to lie beside me. He doesn't ask my permission, no final checks or further molly-coddling. No, we're well beyond that now. He stops only long enough to grab a condom from the drawer beside the bed, snap open the wrapper and unroll it along his length. Then, with no further ado or fanfare, he simply spreads my legs and positions himself between them. He eases the head of his cock into my thoroughly prepared and disgracefully ready entrance, and thrusts hard. His entire length plunges inside me. Easily, deeply, totally. Embedded to the hilt, Nicholas Hardisty stops, holds still, allows me the few moments I need to adjust, to stretch and shape myself around him, to accept his invading presence. My eyes are closed, my head tilted back in silent ecstasy as I savor this moment. I open them slowly, and he's there, looking down into my face, waiting for my signal that it's okay to continue.

I lift my right hand, but only to loop it behind his neck and pull his face toward me. He allows me to pull him down, and I stretch up to kiss his mouth. And that is signal enough. He starts to thrust, at first slowly, withdrawing then re-entering me. I'm tight, I know it, I can feel it. And so can he, and he appears to love it. I'm not so sure, he feels huge, wide and thick and so very hard, and as he forces his length inside me, my body stretches helplessly around him. He's not hurting me, although I'm still nervous, still slightly tense.

He continues to slide into me, then withdraw before filling me again, his full length entering me more easily with each thrust. I know he's treating me very gently and soon my body relaxes, accepts him. He obviously feels the moment my doubts and any remaining resistance borne of inexperience melt away and he picks up the pace, thrusting more quickly, harder, deeper. He lifts my knees, his elbows hooked beneath them to allow himself a better angle, to penetrate me more deeply. This isn't my first time, I'm no virgin, but it's not exactly familiar territory either. He knows it, and I know he's spent a long, long time preparing me. But now, his initial penetration accomplished, he's fucking me hard, offering no respite, no quarter, no further concession to my inexperience. Not that I want that, not anymore. What I'm getting is perfect. Absolutely perfect.

He's filling me and stretching me, and my pussy is starting to clench wildly as the sensations build. Each thrust is perfectly angled, hitting that most sensitive inner spot each time, and just to make sure I get the message, he slips his hand between us to once more position his thumb over my clit. He rubs the swollen, sensitive little nub, hard, matching the rhythm to his thrusts, and my body convulses in orgasm yet again. I can do no more than hang onto his neck, my legs clasped around his waist as he fucks me into total and truly wonderful oblivion. I've heard of being fucked senseless and thought it was just something people said. Now I know better. Now I know what senseless really means. It means this—detachment, this total surrender to the physical, the here and now where nothing else of any importance exists. I genuinely think if the bed beneath us had caught fire I'd have simply shrugged, intending to get around to seeing to it later on. Probably. Much later.

"Come for me again, Freya. Now."

His whispered instruction is none the less commanding, and, incredibly, I find myself obeying. The sensations, which had been subsiding—well, I think they may have been—suddenly erupt in fury once more as another storm of sensation hurls me back into this moment, shuddering, gasping and squeezing him with my inner walls as my body gives up yet another frenzied release. I'm spinning, crazily out of control, my center of gravity scrambled as my body is tossed around in the heady whirlwind. This time though, he's with me, his own release now imminent as I climb once more to that place which has become delightfully familiar to me this evening. And as my pussy tightens and squeezes him hard before eventually relaxing, his muttered oath, more a growl than words signals his climax and I feel the warmth as his semen spurts out to fill the small sac at the end of the condom. He plunges deep, holding that position as his cock twitches, pulses and empties inside me, his arms rigid, tense, as he takes his weight and mine as I wrap myself tightly around him.

Then it's done, and he relaxes, rolling swiftly to his side and pulling me with him so I land on top. I'm pathetically grateful for his consideration. I hadn't expected him to collapse onto me and crush me exactly, but I did wonder…

I lie motionless on top of him, my limp body draped across Nicholas Hardisty's lean chest and hard thighs. I'm intensely conscious of his firm, sculpted length under me, and I want to sink into him, remain part of him as he's become a part of me. He's still inside me, and that joining feels wonderfully intimate to me in those moments as our heart rates calm, dropping from frantic, needy thumping to a soft, sated, rhythmic pulsing. I'm in no hurry to separate from him as our bodies return to normal, this—connection—feels so right to me, and I can't recall ever feeling so deeply contented.

Not so Mr Hardisty, it would seem, and all too soon he shifts, his palms on my hips as he gently lifts me from him. He rolls away, removing the condom and efficiently knotting the open end. He directs a brief smile at me as he slides from the bed, strolling in all his wonderfully naked glory across the room to the en suite in the corner. I hear the flush as he disposes of the condom, then re-emerges to walk back across the room. I try not to stare, honestly I do. But he is absolutely stunning. Tall, hard, all angular planes and toned, corded muscle. I have no idea what he does for a living—maybe I could ask him…? But I'm betting he doesn't spend his time in an office. Those muscles didn't become so perfectly honed in a gym. And then there's the pretty much all over tan. I'm scrutinizing him carefully, yes, definitely staring despite my best intentions. He's slightly paler across his firm, perfectly rounded buttocks, but only very slightly. He clearly spends a great deal of his time outdoors, and not much of it around here. The north west of England is nice enough, but not widely renowned for its sub-tropical climate.

If I'm honest, I don't as a rule think nudity is especially flattering for a man. Clothes do tend to disguise any slightly flabby areas very effectively, and all those dangly bits can be very distracting if you're trying to hold a serious conversation. Not that conversation is high on my 'to do' list just now. And come to think of it, fully naked Doms are a rare enough sight even in a BDSM club. Usually that degree of exposure is reserved for we submissives who are frequently paraded around nude. But Nicholas Hardisty seems to make his own rules, and I am definitely appreciating the view just now.

He strides over to the door leading into the corridor, opens it and steps outside, quite oblivious to the display he's about to gift to any fortunate passerby in the corridor. He's back in a moment, carrying a tray. He returns to the bed and dumps the tray next to me before sitting down himself.

"Room service came. Coffee?"

I scramble into a sitting position, equally unembarrassed to enjoy a naked late night snack and nod my thanks. Apart from a tall carafe of coffee, milk and a bowl of those rough-cut sugar lumps you sometimes see in up-market Italian bistro's, the tray carries a selection of dips along with bowls of vegetable chunks and a plate of still-warm strips of pitta bread. Very healthy, just the sort of food I like. How did he know? Lucky guess, must have been. He turns the two cups on the tray upright and pours coffee into each, again very un-Dom-like. 'Serving' of any sort is normally strictly reserved for submissives or the club staff. Doms lift nothing, unless you count whips, of course.

He hands me a cup, gesturing to me to help myself to milk and sugar. I just take the milk, and settle back against the bed head to sip my coffee. Nicholas Hardisty shifts around to arrange himself next to me, one long, tanned leg bent at the knee and the other stretched out lazily. I can't resist a surreptitious peek at his now less than impressive erection, wondering what sort of provocation it might take to re-kindle it. Maybe later. Hopefully…

We sip in companionable silence for a few minutes, until Nicholas reaches for the now half empty carafe and offers me a refill. I accept, and we repeat the pouring and milk ritual.

"Fancy a nibble?" He lifts the tray and pulls it closer, carefully balancing it across our knees. "Please don't scoff all the hummus—I intend to lick that off your nipples a little later. But you're welcome to anything else…"

My nipples! Christ! I feel my face burning—despite this evening's dizzying succession of intimacies I'm not beyond embarrassment it would appear, and he chuckles softly. "It's playtime, sweetheart, and now that we've started to widen your horizons a little, I'm nowhere near finished with you yet. I'm thinking maybe we could try some of this garlic mayonnaise on your clit too. Unless you're in a hurry to get away, obviously…?

I shake my head, my expression no doubt somewhat dazed. He chooses not to comment, just nods briefly and helps himself to a carrot stick. He dunks it in the garlic mayonnaise, perhaps intending to start developing a taste for the stuff. I can but hope. But he holds it out to me instead, and I obediently open my mouth for him to pop it in.

"Good girl. Now, eat up. You'll be needing your strength."

Chapter Five

He's right of course. I do indeed need my strength.

Nicholas Hardisty takes charge of the food, taking a mouthful for himself, then offering me the same. We clear the carrots and celery first, by mutual agreement our joint favorite, then move on to polish off the pitta. I prefer wholemeal and he seems to favor the white stuff, but otherwise we're in total accord. The hummus remains untouched, but we make short work of the taramasalata and some sort of cheesy chivey thing. At last all the nibbles are gone, and Nicholas stands to shift the tray, placing it on the floor by the door. He brings the tub of hummus back and places it on the bedside table, along with the remaining garlic mayonnaise. His dark gray gaze is warm as he watches my reaction. I try for cool, I really do, but fail miserably. I can feel my pussy becoming wet just at the thought of what's to come, and he bloody knows it.

Smiling softly he reaches for the hummus and places the small pot in my right hand, kindly refraining from commenting overmuch on my trembling fingers and the fact that I almost drop the lot.

"Hold tight, love. Don't want to spill it, do we? Now, in a moment I'd like you to cover your nipples with this stuff, and then present your breasts to me. Do you know how to do that? Present your breasts, I mean?

I shake my head, a small frown on my face. And he's no longer smiling. This might be playtime, but we're back to Dom/sub stuff now and that's serious, sort of. He means me to obey him, and to do this right.

"You'll kneel, in front of me, on the bed. Usually you'd do this standing up, but since we're here… Anyway, you'll fold your arms behind your back, cup each elbow with the opposite hand. That pulls your shoulders back and pushes your breasts out. Very pretty. You do have beautiful breasts, by the way. Did I mention that?"

Beautiful breasts? Me? Well I always quite liked them but no one else has ever commented. I could really get to like Nicholas Hardisty.

"But that's enough of you fishing for compliments, Miss Stone. Get on with it please." His formal, clipped tone seems incongruous given the light, teasing banter, but I know it's deliberate. This is fun, we're here to enjoy ourselves together. We're here to indulge ourselves in fucking good sex with a generous dose of kink thrown in, but he's the top and I'm the bottom, and we both know the rules.

He holds my gaze for a few moments more, then I give in first and drop my eyes. I focus on the pot of innocent-looking hummus and with no further ado scoop a generous helping onto the fingers of my left hand. My eyes now firmly fixed on my breasts, and more particularly my right nipple, I carefully apply the creamy, grainy substance to my body, making sure the nipple is completely covered before transferring the pot to my right hand and repeating the process with my left nipple. I'm generous, leaving no part of the rosy tips uncovered. Luckily the hummus is thick and sticky, and stays put very obligingly. Once I'm satisfied with my work I pick up a serviette from the tray and wipe my fingers, taking my time before shifting into a more formal kneeling position, and arranging my arms behind my back as instructed.

He's right, the position does exactly what he said it would. The effect is decadent, salacious even. And doing it, inviting his attention in this way, I feel like a total slut. Deliciously, blatantly sluttish. Wonderful.

He's lying on the bed, his shoulders propped against the headboard as he watches me. "That's very good, little sub. For your first attempt. Now, come closer please."

I shuffle forward on my knees, careful not to topple over as the unnatural position of my arms throws me off balance. I definitely don't want to waste all that lovely hummus by wiping it all over the bedclothes.

"Straddle me." The command is issued in a low tone, quiet but clear.

I obey without hesitation. Or try to. I almost over-balance when I lift my left knee to reach over him, but he makes no move to steady me, just sits still, his eyes on my breasts. I let go of my careful positioning momentarily, but quickly settle down astride his stomach and restore order.

"You'll need to practice that. When you're presenting your breasts to me, you don't release your arms, not for any reason, unless I give you permission to do so. That's to be your only warning, sub. Is there anything about my instructions that you don't completely understand?"

I shake my head, all nervous anticipation now. All hint of playfulness is gone, Nicholas Hardisty is in total Dom mode, and absolutely terrifying. And exciting. Powerful. Thrilling. Irresistible. He reaches out his right hand to cup the underside of my left breast, lifting the soft globe slightly, testing the weight. His fingers are gentle, his touch light. It surprises me, I'd expected him to be more…severe. But he's full of surprises, his handling of me soft and caring. Tender almost.

"Lean forward, and place your breast in my mouth. Do it slowly, please."

I draw a slow, shaky breath, and do as I'm told.

My pussy clenches delightfully as Nicholas Hardisty's tongue curls around my nipple. The sensitive nub has grown and hardened under the hummus, and by the time he takes it in his mouth and sucks, hard, I'm beyond aroused. My position straddling his body makes sure my engorged clitoris and labia are in contact with his naked stomach which in turn ensures he's under no illusions regarding my growing arousal as my juices flow freely. My whole body is tingling, desperate for release, for anything, and I find that I can angle my body slightly to create the friction I'm by now absolutely craving against my clit. I try to do so only to have him growl at me.

"No taking control, little sub. Your clit can wait. Unless you'd like me to clamp it for you…?"

Christ, no! I shake my head desperately, and make it my business to remember to sit still, no matter what he does to me.

"Thought not. Don't interrupt again. Now, where was I?"

He quickly finds his place again, taking my nipple and much of my breast into his mouth before lapping lazily at it until all the hummus is gone and I'm panting with need. He uses his hands to lift and shape my breast, holding it in exactly the right position for his ministrations to have best effect, and I can do nothing but remain still, my arms clasped uncomfortably behind my back, all my senses focused on what he's doing to me.

Eventually he lifts his gaze to mine again. "The other one now, please."

He waits patiently for the few seconds it takes me to reposition myself, bringing my right breast toward his mouth. Again, he takes its weight in his hand, lifting my breast to place it exactly where he wants it in order to repeat the sensuous torture. He starts by curling just his tongue around the nipple, scooping away the hummus before flicking it lightly. Then he opens his mouth to draw more of my breast in, stroking it lightly with his fingers as he uses his lips and teeth to tease the soft, responsive curves, licking away all the creamy goo to leave my skin gleaming and clean. I gasp, my body clenching under the onslaught, but I can't help that. I hope he won't take issue, especially as I can feel my slick juices smearing his stomach. God, how obvious. Such a slut. If I hadn't already had God knows how many orgasms in the last couple of hours, I'd come again, just from the skilled pressure of his tongue on my nipples, but I'm already well sated and made of sterner stuff by now it seems. Still, there's always the garlic mayo to fall back on.

"You can move your arms now, Freya." He lifts his gaze to mine again, still caressing my breast lazily with his palm, shaping and molding it in his hand.

I wait for the squeeze, the pinch or twist at my nipple, but it doesn't come. He's all gentle, all tender care. Reverent almost.

"Beautiful. Soft and round, and just fits in my hand. And your nipples are so responsive. You make my mouth water, Miss Stone, you really do. And talking of which, lie back and spread your legs please."

Ah yes, the mayonnaise…

I lie back obediently and lift my knees, letting my legs fall open obligingly. Nicholas kneels on the floor, placing his hands on my hips to position me at the edge of the bed. Unresisting, I allow him to maneuver me into position, and I wait.

"Now you present your clit to me. Do you know how to do that?"

Again I shake my head, and I wait for my instructions.

"You use the index and middle fingers of each of your hands to part the lips, exposing your clitoris and making sure it's totally accessible for me. You spread the lips wide and hold them open, even if it feels uncomfortable. And as before, you hold perfectly still, whatever I do to you. Is that clear?"

I nod briefly, but it's enough.

"No questions?"

I shake my head this time.

"Fine. Do it then, please."

I reach down, carefully placing the fingers of each hand as he described, and pull the lips surrounding my clitoris apart. I'm slippery, slick with my own juices, and it's not easy to grip. And I have a distinct suspicion it won't be getting any easier any time soon.

"Mmm, looking good, Miss Stone. You have a very pretty little cunt there. And your clit is positively throbbing. Are you rather excited, perhaps, Freya?"

I close my eyes, my head tilted back. Christ, I just want him to touch me. I need to come so much, so badly now. Or better still maybe we could skip all this foreplay palaver and he could just fuck me again. Please. What's with all the chat?

"Answer me. A simple nod will do. Are you a little bit excited, Miss Stone? Aroused, perhaps? Or are you just wishing I'd get on with it and fuck you again?"

Christ, that bloody telepathy. I nod, but keep my eyes tightly closed. I feel so exposed, lying in front of him like this. My clitoris and pussy are blatantly laid open for him to study and to comment on, even if he is complimentary, appreciative and terribly polite. I'm totally vulnerable, and closing my eyes seems to offer me some illusion of privacy.

But it is an illusion, and a dangerous one. I jerk violently as the cool mayonnaise connects with my hot, throbbing clit, smoothed and spread there by his gentle fingers.

"Keep still, Miss Stone. I'll let that little wriggle go because this stuff's cold and you weren't expecting it, but you do not move again. Is that clear? And if you don't want to be taken by surprise, I suggest you open your eyes."

I manage to prize my eyelids apart, and glance up at him. His slate-colored eyes are gleaming, his own arousal obvious as he lowers his gaze to once more examine my sensitive clit, now generously daubed with aromatic salad dressing. He dips his head, slowly nibbling his way along my inner right thigh and across my straining fingers to touch the tip of his tongue delicately into the mayonnaise on the inner lips. Only by extreme force of will do I manage to remain still.

"Good girl, you're learning. Now let's try that again."

This time he trails his tongue the length of my left thigh, and again I manage to anchor myself to the bed as he dips his tongue into the mayonnaise coating the very edge of my clit. There's nothing at all I can do, though, to stem the flow of my juices, and I just know my clit is swelling even before his eyes. He slants a storm-gray glance back up at me, smiling softly. "This isn't going to take long, is it, my beautiful little slut? You're going to come as soon as my tongue touches your clit. You'll be going off like a little firecracker, won't you? And I'm going to watch, and enjoy the show. And, Freya, you need to concentrate because I want you to hold that position, until I've removed every last bit of mayonnaise and I tell you you can move. Okay?"

He expects an answer, and I nod, desperate by then for this to be over. I find myself wondering if it's possible to actually die of pleasure? Or of terrible anticipation? I only have a few brief moments to ponder these great questions before he drops his head again, this time fastening his lips around my engorged clit and sucking hard. And he's absolutely right, I do go off like a firecracker. The rush of orgasm is instantaneous, engulfing me, hitting me like a tsunami. I'm drowning in it, shuddering and trembling under the onslaught, but somehow I manage to obey his instructions. I hold the position, maintaining my death grip on my slick folds, holding my body exposed and accessible as he licks, sucks, nibbles my quivering clit and I shake helplessly underneath him. My breath is catching, hitching in my throat, the only sound to betray the depth of my surrender to this sensual attack. Nothing so far has compared to this. This is total and absolute surrender, and he completely owns my response.

He takes his time, drawing out the ecstasy as the electrifying buzz of my release washes over and through me, every nerve ending tingling, focused entirely on that little bud of sizzling, throbbing flesh gripped so mercilessly between Nicholas Hardisty's lips.

At last, at long last, the shocks and after-shocks subside and my body drifts unsteadily back into the here and now. As I regain some semblance of consciousness of my surroundings I realize I'm still holding the position. Incredibly, the force of his will is stronger than even the most powerful orgasm. I obey him, despite everything.

"Good girl. Let me take over now." He peels my rigid fingers away, placing my hands by my sides on the bed. Then he replaces my fingers with his own, stroking, exploring, testing.

He slides three fingers inside me, easily, my pussy ready and welcoming, the walls clenching and grasping him. I want, need, him to fill me. Now. If I had a voice I'd beg, but as it is I can only hope he'll get the message.

He does. Of course he does. That bloody telepathy for once on my side. "God, you're lovely when you're so aroused. You want me inside you, don't you? Tell me what you want, Freya. Can you remember the signal?"

I think for a moment then squeeze my inner muscles hard, the signal that says 'I like this, I want more'.

"Turn over. I'm fucking you from behind this time. You did say that was your favorite, and you've been so good that I'm taking requests." He stands, flips me over onto my stomach, and quickly positions me with my knees bent and my bum in the air.

He shoves my knees apart as far as they'll go and kneels behind me. There's a tear of the condom foil pack opening, and I wait a couple of seconds for him to unroll the latex. Then his hands are on me. This time he uses his thumbs to gently part the lips of my pussy as he carefully positions the head of his cock in my entrance. He waits for a moment, steadying me, before plunging deep, filling me completely.

I'm ready, totally ready and expecting it, but still I gasp. He just takes my breath away, every time. He starts to thrust, long and sure and firm, with each stroke burying himself to the hilt inside my unresisting body. It's wonderful, each thrust of his cock perfectly positioned to connect with that oh-so-sensitive spot inside me, with unerring precision, a direct hit every time. And he also leans in, reaching under me to place the pad of his finger on my clit, stroking lightly, in time with his rhythmic momentum. And it's that gesture of unselfish sensuality, done for no other reason than to heighten my pleasure, that tips me once more into the boiling turmoil of orgasm. Suddenly I'm spinning, swirling— my senses again scrambling as my body clenches in desperate release, grabbing and gripping him, the feeling of fullness heightened as my pussy convulses around him. He uses his finger on my clit to increase the pressure, circling and rubbing as I claw at the bedding beneath me, my hands curling into fists as I crest yet another glorious wave.

Nicholas Hardisty's own muffled curse of pleasure tells me that he has come too. I suspect I've had the best of this bargain, to be fair. In fact, I've lost count of how many times I've come this evening, but he's doing all right too. And that realization fills me with a sense of pure female satisfaction. It's been a wonderful learning curve for me, even the not so nice bits at the beginning, but I've managed to give Nicholas Hardisty a good time too. Who would have thought it?

It's over. This most wonderful, sensual, unexpected turn of events is coming to a close. This most perfect evening is almost at an end. He has to go. Real life can always be relied on to upturn even the sturdiest of apple carts, and this evening is no exception.

"I have to make a trip tomorrow. Today in fact. I need to be checking in at Manchester in four hours so I'm going to have to go soon. I have to pick up my passport and some other stuff." He does look genuinely regretful as he hands me a warm, wet flannel to wipe off any remaining bits of stickiness from my breasts and watches my progress carefully as I apply it. Then, "How are you getting home, Freya?"

I pass the flannel back to him and mimic driving, using my hands to grip and turn a pretend steering wheel, and he nods. "Where are you parked? In the car park around the back?"

Now it's my turn to nod.

"Good. Get dressed and I'll see you to your car. You *are* okay to drive, aren't you?"

Who would have thought it, I am. I actually am. After everything, I'm perfectly happy to hop into my car and drive myself home. Summer was fretting over nothing.

Oh shit! Oh, God! Summer! It's been hours since I left her in the bar downstairs, and I've not given her another thought until now. Christ, she'll be frantic. I'll be lucky if she hasn't called the police, declared me dead, or missing, or at the very least dangerously deranged. I leap to my feet, grab my skirt from the floor over by the door, start to drag it on.

"Whoah, what's the rush? I'm the one with a plane to catch."

Nicholas has just zipped up his jeans and he's working on turning his shirt the right way out as I launch into my headless chicken impression. I rush back to the bed, rummaging frantically around in the tangled sheets for his phone. Finding it, I fumble for the on switch, only to have him gently, calmly, take it from me, turn it on and hand it back with the notepad app fired up.

My friend. I came with a friend. She's downstairs, been waiting for me all this time.

I shove the phone back at him, and continue to wrestle with my top.

"No, she left hours ago. Dan put her in a taxi." His quiet response stuns me into immobility.

What? I gape at him, incredulous. *Dan? Daniel? That other Dom, the one Summer, delusional as she is, thought was the better looking of the two? A taxi? What the hell? Why?*

So much for coherent thinking.

"They spent a couple of hours together, he managed to convince her that you'd come to no lasting harm, and that she could safely leave you with me." All my confusion must be plastered all over my face, so Nicholas kindly helps out with a bit more explanation. "And he put her in a taxi at around one o'clock. She'll be tucked up in bed by now."

I continue to stare at him, and he gently takes the phone back from my fingers. He taps the screen to bring up his text messages, and shows me the one from his friend Dan Praed, received just before midnight, asking if I was still with him. He scrolls down, showing me his response, that I was with him and we'd be a while yet. Dan's response to that was that Summer was ready to leave and he'd sort out a taxi for her. And he asked Nicholas to let me know she'd left.

"Sorry, I got the text while we were still down in the dungeon. You were—preoccupied—and I completely forgot about it until now."

I shake my head, totally bemused. Summer and that, that—individual—spent a couple of hours together! Doing what for Christ's sake? I dread to think. Innocent, upstanding, prim and perfectly proper Summer spent 'a couple of hours' in a fetish club with a Dom. My God, what did he do to her? Surely he wouldn't…

Nicholas Hardisty catches my startled face between his palms, leaning in close. "Don't look so stricken. If she spent the evening with Dan, you can be sure she enjoyed herself. You can ask her tomorrow. Today. Whatever. Anyway, are you ready? Did you bring a coat? A bag?"

I nod, still reeling from the revelations about Summer, not able to think quite straight. No matter, Nicholas Hardisty is in charge as usual. "Right, cloakroom first, and then I'll walk you to your car." He strolls to the door, holding out his hand.

I take it, and follow him out into the corridor.

My head's still churning with bizarre images of Summer embroiled in Christ knows what, with God only knows who, and I can't believe it. She usually gives men a wide berth. Even nice, sedate, safe men. She is definitely not drawn to dangerous Dominant men with whips and canes and a startling penchant for bondage. He must have forced her or…something. But he seemed so nice, so polite. Who'd have thought he could…? I need to talk to her. Soon. Make sure she's all right. And it strikes me how odd this is, it's usually the other way around, Summer checking up on me and helping to sort out my little and not so little dramas.

I keep my anxieties over Summer to myself—I somehow doubt Nicholas Hardisty will share my concern. No words are exchanged as we stroll along the now deserted corridors and down the main stairs toward the front door. The cloakroom is a small kiosk just inside the front entrance, and my long raincoat is the only garment left in there. Although the club is in theory open twenty-four hours a day, in practice most business is done between ten p.m. and two a.m. It's now three thirty a.m. and pretty much everyone else has drifted off. The night attendant passes me my bag and my coat, and I'm a little surprised to see Nicholas take possession of a black motor cycle crash helmet and padded black leather jacket. A biker then, I never knew that. I slip my coat on over my skimpy costume. It's not especially cold outside, or raining, but a long cover up style raincoat just helps to avoid any awkwardness at traffic lights if another motorist happens to catch sight of me. I'm quite sedately dressed this evening, but I often do a nice line in leather and crimson satin and that would raise a few eyebrows if I found myself changing a tire by the roadside or needing to stop for petrol.

I dig in my bag for my phone, check for texts. Sure enough, there's one from Summer. I open it fast.

Sorry I missed u. Going away for a bit. C u soon.

Going away? Why? Where? What the hell? What happened to her?

"May I?" Nicholas is holding out his hand, clearly wanting to see the text. Numb, confused, I hand my phone over to him. He scans the message then glances back at me. "From your expression I guess you didn't know she was planning a trip?"

I'm shaking my head, frowning, confused. And really worried now about my friend.

"It's too late to find out anything more now, but I'll check with Dan tomorrow if you like, and let you know how she was when she left here. And if she told him anything about going away. Okay?"

He tips my chin up and smiles at me, and my stomach does one of those little flips it's been practicing all evening. He really is incredibly beautiful, and I desperately want him to be my Dom. Just for a little bit longer. Or maybe just occasionally — I'll take what I can get.

Instinctively I start to sign the word 'please', only to find Nicholas' smartphone back in my hands. I manage to find the notepad app for myself, and quickly write my last plea.

Please, won't you reconsider? Not for money, just for

Nicholas doesn't let me finish. Folding his hands around mine, he stops my scribbling. I look up at him, knowing what his answer will be. He's smiling at me, a little sadly now, but I know he means what he says.

"I'm sorry, but no. That's my last word, it's not happening. I don't train subs anymore, not in any serious way. And you need someone who'll take a lot of time with you, time that I just don't have. If it's any consolation though, I've really enjoyed your company this evening. Really, seriously enjoyed it. You are beautiful, responsive, and you'll make a wonderful submissive. Remember everything I told you, Freya, everything you did learn tonight, and hang on to the wristbands. They should come in useful. And if we meet up here in the future, I'd love to scene with you again. If you want to…?"

If I want to? In that moment I know I don't want to submit for anyone else. Not ever. If he won't teach me, then I just won't be learning. There would be no point. I nod, finally accepting that at best I'll have occasional evenings with Nicholas Hardisty, if I'm lucky. And meanwhile he'll probably be having a great time topping other much more experienced and rewarding subs, and eventually he'll forget about me. He shrugs into his own leather jacket and tucks the helmet under his left arm. Slipping his right arm across my shoulders, he turns me toward the exit. We walk slowly down the front steps of the big old converted house and crunch our way around the graveled path toward the large car parking area at the rear of the building. The only cars there now are mine and a couple of staff vehicles, and I spot what must be Nicholas' motor bike close to the entrance. It's a huge black beast, looks very powerful, suits him really.

Sure enough, he dumps the helmet on the seat of the motor bike and asks me which is my car. I point to my pride and joy, a rather lovely—even if I do say so myself—maroon red Aston Martin Vanquish, and I feel rather than hear the sharp intake of breath.

"Shit, that's some serious car. Yours?" The incredulity in his voice is strangely satisfying—at least now he might believe me that I could have laid my hands on the twenty-five thousand I offered him.

I simply nod, and walk toward it, the keyless sensor in my bag unlocking the driver's door with a welcoming click as I approach. The headlights come on automatically too, illuminating the entire car park.

Nicholas is walking slowly around my shiny toy, viewing it from every angle, all admiring whistles and perplexed expression. I just stand and wait, and eventually he's back beside me, shaking his head in bewilderment. Now this he definitely did not expect. And I'm perversely glad to have at last succeeded in stunning him into silence.

"That's one seriously lovely car, Freya. What did you say you do for a living?"

Naturally, I don't answer.

"Freya?" he hands me the phone again. "How come you're driving this? It must be worth around two hundred grand..."

£189,950. I bought it three months ago. Do you like it?

"Yes, I fucking like it. But how...?"

I won the lottery.

And on that bombshell I decide to leave him. I hand him his phone back, flash him a brief smile and slip into my car. He's still watching me in amazement as I press the launch control button to switch on the ignition and smoothly purr out of the car park. I'm trying for a dignified exit, and I think I hit the spot.

Chapter Six

The drive from Lancaster, where the Collared and Tied club is, to Kendal, where I live, normally takes about an hour, but at this time the M6 is clear and I can put my foot down. The purr of the Vanquish is barely audible, even at upwards of eighty miles an hour, and I have to keep telling myself to slow down. Supercars like this one are tempting targets for motorway police and I don't want to be stopped. I'm not dressed for it, despite my sensible mac. I just want to get home and lock myself in my apartment for a few days—or maybe weeks—to savor my memories, lick my wounds and generally get over this evening.

And I need to chase up Summer. I haven't forgotten her, and maybe this Dan will be able to shed some light on that. But I have a more pressing problem.

I'm in love. I know it, I don't know how, but I just know it down to my toe nails. Tonight, I fell in love with Nicholas Hardisty. And he doesn't give a shit about me. Well, not much of one. He likes me well enough, enjoyed fucking me and apparently wouldn't mind doing it again sometime. But I'd need a lot of work, and he hasn't gotten time for me. That hurts, even though I know I'm not entitled to expect anything of him. He made me no promises and if I'm honest he didn't seem in the least bothered really about whether or not he saw me again. Despite his kind words as we collected our coats, it was obvious by the time I drove off that he was a great deal more impressed with my car than he was with me.

Shit, what a mess!

It's four twenty in the morning as I let myself into my apartment by the River Kent, just on the outskirts of Kendal town center. It's a lovely spot, and I bought this place soon after the Euromillions cash hit my bank account. It was the first thing I bought in fact.

I could have moved away, could have gone anywhere I liked I suppose. But I like it here. I grew up in Cumbria, in a less salubrious part of it to be fair. Downtown Barrow-in-Furness is not exactly an idyllic spot. My first home was in an industrial wasteland made up of grotty, corrugated, pre-fabricated workshops and warehouses and tiny workers' cottages. After my parents died, when I was about three, me and my gran lived in one of those little cottages. It was tiny but big enough for just the two of us. I loved it because I could walk to the seawall from our house and I could stand looking out across the sandy flatlands of Morecambe Bay and imagine it was the Sahara desert. Or a lunar landscape perhaps. A ten-year-old's imagination has no boundaries, no limits.

Which is more than can be said for the life span of an elderly woman with a forty a day habit and lung cancer. My gran became ill when I was ten. She coughed a lot, but she always had and at first I took no notice. But she lost weight as well, and became so tired she was often still in bed when I got home from school. And still my ten-year-old brand of relentless optimism told me it would pass, no need to worry, old people were like that sometimes. Then the doctor started coming, and he came a lot. My gran rarely got out of bed, and nurses started arriving too. I got into the habit of cooking my own tea, and getting myself up for school, and still I clung on to the notion that things would be fine. They had to be fine. There was no alternative. It was just me and Gran, so she couldn't be really ill. Could she?

But she could, and she was, and eventually the day came that she had to go into the hospital. And she was never coming out. She knew it, and somewhere at the back of my ten-year-old mind, in that place where I'd buried the truth because it was too awful to look at, I knew it too. And Mrs Johnson, the social worker who came to pick me up as the ambulance pulled away around the corner of our street with my gran in the back, certainly knew it. She was very kind and sweet, and she tried hard. Too hard. She was a lot too jolly for my liking, and she explained that I needed someone to look after me now, until something could be worked out. She was careful not to suggest my gran might get better, that I might go home again to our little two-up two-down near the sea in Barrow. Instead, she dropped me off at a large house in Ulverston, handed me over to a motherly woman by the name of Margaret, and told me she'd be back to see me soon.

The social worker did come back. Once or twice. She always asked me how I was, and if I'd been to see my gran at all. It was Margaret though who actually took me to the hospital, then to the hospice where my gran was spending her final weeks. It was Margaret who sat beside her bed with me for hours at a time.

And it was Margaret who came into my bedroom in the middle of the night and whispered to me that I had to get dressed and come with her. It was Margaret who explained that there'd been a call from the hospice and we should go there now. I was shaking as we drove in silence through the thick, deepest darkness that comes before dawn, the ten miles or so to the quiet, peaceful hospice on the outskirts of Kendal. My gran's personal carer was waiting for us and welcomed us inside, ushering us quickly to my gran's small, cheerful room, more like a cozy hotel than a hospital. Margaret told me I didn't have to go into the room if I didn't want to, but that she really thought I should. I did too, however awful the next few hours were going to be. And I trusted Margaret by then, so I nodded and reached for her hand. The carer left us there, murmuring that she'd be close by if we needed her.

It was Margaret who sat with me at my gran's bedside for the final two hours of her life, and it was Margaret's gentle hands on my shoulders that lent me the courage to smile when my gran briefly opened her eyes for the last time. She looked straight at me, then at Margaret with an expression close to pleading. By then, though, my gran was well beyond the point she could have any further effect on my future, and as she closed her eyes for the last time, I sensed that she let me go. And it was Margaret who held me as I sobbed when my gran finally, mercifully, stopped breathing.

I was to learn later how Margaret had agonized over that decision, over whether to wake me up and take me to the hospice to see my gran that last time, but eventually she'd decided I should have the chance to say goodbye. She was right, of course. Margaret was still there, holding my hand at my gran's funeral, attended only by the two of us, by Mrs Johnson and a couple of my gran's old friends from when she'd worked at Woolworth's in Barrow town center. And it was Margaret who eventually took me home again to her lovely old house in Ulverston and let me cry in my room for two days.

On the third day she came into my room, and this time didn't just leave me some food on a tray, give me a little cuddle and leave. This time she sat down on my bed, made me sit up, and she wiped my eyes with tissues. I tried to push her away, I wasn't ready yet, but she was having none of it.

"I can't even start to imagine how you're feeling, sweetheart, so you'll have to tell me. Eventually, if you want to. But just in case you're wondering, if it might help, I want you to know you have a home here, with me, for as long as you need it. You can stay with me for good, or if you want I could ask Mrs Johnson at social services to look for a different long-term foster place for you. If there's somewhere else you'd rather live…?"

I remember I gazed at her, through my swollen, red and tear-filled eyes. She looked all hazy and blurred, as if I were watching her through a glass of water, and utterly, utterly wonderful. Even though I didn't really expect to be allowed to stay with her, over the weeks I'd spent in her big, rambling old house I'd not been able to help loving her. Just a little, because she was so kind. And because she cuddled me a lot and made me nice food every day. But I was sure they'd make me move—I thought she'd want me gone to make room for some other little kid who needed her more than I did. So at first I couldn't believe it, couldn't take it in.

Did she mean what it sounded like? That I wasn't in the way, that if I wanted to I could stay?

I didn't answer her. I didn't ever tell her I wanted to stay. I just stayed. And stayed and stayed and stayed. Until a year had gone by, then another year. Other children had come and gone during that time, but I just stayed.

When she wasn't rescuing sad and lonely little girls Margaret was a quilter. She made beautiful, intricate quilts out of tiny pieces of fabric, most of which she designed herself. She made quilts as presents for people, for exhibitions, for special occasions. And she taught me how to make them too. It's a wonderful, restful pastime, and I love being able to take a pile of worthless looking scraps of cotton and work them into something stunning. It's something else I can do in silence, on level terms with any other quilter. With Margaret I made quilts for shows and I won prizes, became quite well known in our little circle.

The years rolled smoothly by, and I was settled with Margaret. I went on to secondary school, where they gave me a dedicated tutor all for me, because I was so 'special'. I couldn't speak, and as if that wasn't bad enough, I was 'looked after' as well. One time I saw the phrase 'multiple disadvantages' on a report in my tutor's file on me, and I wondered who she was writing about and how this other kid's papers had gotten into my file. I never felt disadvantaged, and surely being 'looked after' is a good thing? It definitely is if the looking after is done by Margaret Maloney, who eventually filled in the forms and formally adopted me when I was fourteen.

I've never called her 'mum' and I never will. She'll always be Margaret as far as I'm concerned. But she means the world to me and that won't change, even though she now lives in New South Wales with George. George, short for Georgina, is an Australian restaurant owner she met on holiday in Tunisia a couple of years after I moved in with her. The two women hit it off and corresponded endlessly after they returned home. They continued to meet once or twice a year in various exotic parts of the globe over the years that followed, often with me in tow. It took me a while to work out the true nature of their relationship, but by the time the penny dropped, I adored George and it never occurred to me that there was anything unusual about their set-up. They finally formalized their civil partnership a couple of years ago, and Margaret moved to Sydney. I suspect she'd have emigrated a lot sooner but for me. She wouldn't leave me, wouldn't uproot me, and she steadfastly put me first. It wasn't until I hit the Euromillions jackpot, and moved out of her house in Ulverston to take up residence in my own fancy apartment that she finally put up the for sale sign and made arrangements to move Down Under.

Unfortunately by then the credit crunch had put a stop to pretty much all house sales, and Margaret was stuck here in the UK, waiting for a buyer who wouldn't be materializing any time soon. I loved her and I didn't want her to move half a world away, but I knew she'd stood her watch as far as I was concerned, so I bought her house. I did the deal through my lawyer and an agent—she never knew it was me who cut the last tie holding her here. She's always flatly and absolutely refused to accept any share of my winnings so I had no choice but to keep a low profile. But now she's happy, doing front of house stuff in George's restaurant, and I visit them when I get the urge. Which is pretty often.

Winning the Euromillions lottery absolutely floored me. I was only just nineteen then, and bought the ticket on impulse. It's the one and only time I ever did buy one. How mad is that?

I was still living in Ulverston with Margaret and at college trying to top up my meager stash of A levels. I left school with a few GCSEs and an A level in English Literature, not enough to get me into university, and in any case I wasn't convinced that was the right route for me. At that time I had no real idea of what I wanted to do, but I loved cooking and was vaguely wondering about a career in catering. I had a dream of running my own little tearoom or guest house, and having grown up in an area overrun by tourists for most of the year, I naturally assumed I could make a living in the hospitality industry somewhere. I had my sights set on catering college eventually, once I'd met the entry requirements, and would probably have done all right, but events took another course for me.

I didn't even properly understand the Euromillions system, and in fairness I'd gotten it all a bit confused with the Camelot set-up. I thought I was on the look-out for six balls and the Bonus Ball. I checked the result of the National Lottery draw that weekend and couldn't work out why there wasn't mention of main numbers and Lucky Stars. But I'm persistent, I fiddled about online in my bedroom, eventually found the Euromillions site, and bingo! Well, so to speak.

And even then I didn't get it, didn't really understand what I was looking at. The numbers on the screen were mine, exactly the same as mine, all five main numbers and the two Lucky Stars. Estimated jackpot, given it was a rollover week, forty-four million pounds. But it couldn't be true, I convinced myself that somehow my own numbers had gotten entered into my computer system, I must have done it while I was trying to check, and what I was seeing was hypothetical. For hours I steadfastly refused to let myself even start to consider I might have won. I never breathed a word of it to Margaret, just went to bed that night as if everything was quite, quite normal. As if my life was not about to be changed forever.

But I hadn't put my numbers into my computer. I knew, deep down I knew I hadn't done that. So, eventually, curled up in my bed late that night, just before I went to sleep, I logged on again. This time I knew exactly what site to go to, and I concentrated hard. No mistakes, no misunderstandings. I was looking at the actual draw that had taken place the previous day, those actual numbers were the winning ones. And yes, they *were* my numbers. Definitely.

No harm in getting a second opinion though. I texted Summer, my best friend since we were both fifteen and she had shared my bedroom at Margaret's for a few weeks. She was in bed I expect—it was after one in the morning by then I recall—but I typed my message asking her to check the Euromillions website for the most recent draw and text me back the winning numbers. Then I turned off my laptop, and I went to sleep.

The following morning I checked my texts. There was one from Summer. With my numbers in it. I looked again at my ticket, as if the numbers might have somehow magicked themselves into something different overnight, but no, there it was. I was a winner. A big winner. I texted Summer back—I needed her to make some calls for me. And I went downstairs to talk to Margaret.

And the rest is history. With Summer's help, and Margaret's, I claimed my winnings, and soon learned that I was, subject to final checks, proudly in possession of forty-four million, seven hundred and thirty-seven thousand, two hundred and ninety-seven pounds. And a few pence. I opted to keep a low profile, much to the disgust of the company representatives who wanted to make a big splash about me. *'Lottery virgin hits the jackpot at first attempt'* sort of stuff. I wasn't having it, only my close friends and family knew what had happened—Summer, Margaret, George—and apart from staff at my bank and at the lottery itself, I've kept it that way ever since.

As well as buying the old house in Ulverston, which I've since had converted into holiday flats, I treated myself to a lovely home just for me. I wandered into an exclusive estate agency in Lancaster, having been referred to them by my wealth consultant at Lloyds private bank, and explained that I wanted an apartment. My needs were straightforward enough. I was looking for a luxury place, somewhere in Cumbria, the best they could find. No upper price limit. They came up with a list of about six to consider, but my place in Kendal ticked all my boxes. The right size, town center, private spa, gym and pool, not too remote. I loved it as soon as I set foot in it, and it set me back just over one and a half million pounds. A bargain, I thought.

Then I bought myself a decent car. I originally settled for a modestly priced BMW coupe, as I hadn't even passed my test at that stage. I booked some lessons, got myself a provisional license, failed my test twice, but eventually managed to convince the driving examiner I was fit to be let loose. Then I started looking around for something really nice, and I found the Aston Martin Vanquish. Again, it was love at first sight. I ordered one, stumped up my two hundred thousand pounds, then had to wait three months for delivery. It was worth the wait.

The lottery people sent a very nice gentleman called David Carnegie to see me. He's a wealth manager, retained by the Euromillions folk to go round and talk sense into the newly filthy rich. It's David's job to stop us going mad, taking up extreme sports and getting ourselves killed, or giving it all away to the first clever conman that knocks on the door. It's David's job to explain about investment, about financial planning, about avoiding criminals and scroungers, about making gifts to causes that I choose, and about not spending it all at once. In reality, he didn't tell me anything that my gran and Margaret hadn't already drilled into me, just that this time the numbers were big. These numbers had commas in.

At that stage I hadn't yet discovered my submissive side, so Mr Carnegie's exhortations to avoid the more foolhardy pursuits seemed superfluous. I've never harbored any ambition to leap from a perfectly serviceable airplane, or fling myself off a cliff attached to a rubber band. I don't swim that well so there'll be no white water nonsense for me. Quilting seems safe enough.

By way of celebration once I'd sorted out my apartment, I booked a luxury trip to Australia to spend a bit more time with Margaret. First class flights, VIP airport lounges, five star hotels—I splashed out big-style. Just for once it was nice to feel I could have anything I wanted, do anything I wanted, go anywhere I wanted. Except it wasn't, isn't, just for once. It's forever, probably. Forty-four million pounds takes a lot of shifting, especially when you're me and there's nothing, really, you want to buy with it.

At David Carnegie's suggestion, I deposited the balance of my fortune with Lloyds private bank. They were very pleased to see me, especially when it became clear that my winnings were still pretty much intact. They allocated another personal wealth consultant as my adviser, a very serious middle-aged chap by the name of Max Furrowes. Max spent a lot of time with me discussing my attitude to risk, and finally arriving at a 'risk tolerance' diagnosis of medium. That means I don't mind some uncertainty, within reason, but I won't be putting the lot on the three-thirty at York. I did, however, seriously consider buying a racehorse until Max pointed out that this would represent a 'moderate' risk. I don't do moderate, and settled instead for a prudent portfolio of unexciting but workmanlike investments expertly managed by Max and his extremely reliable colleagues at Lloyds. I made a few charitable donations, but by the time I'd exhausted my shopping list, the bank still had over forty-two million pounds of mine to play with, which even conservatively invested returns earnings of over six hundred thousand a year. I worked out that I can live comfortably on a hundred thousand a year, and the rest gets reinvested.

How's that for prudent? Max is definitely impressed.

I loved seeing Margaret again, and my trip to Australia was fabulous. I was delighted that the foster mum I adored was so happy with the love of her life — that said life was turning out as she wanted it to. But after a few weeks basking in the heat of an Australian summer, I knew I wanted to come home, back to the

UK, back to the Lake District where I felt I belonged. And where it's cool most of the time. And wet.

And now, four years on, I shouldn't complain. I have my lovely apartment, more money in the bank than I know what to do with so no need to worry about working for a living. My time's my own, so I do a lot of quilting. I still enter the shows and exhibitions, although it's not nearly as much fun without Margaret to share it with. Despite Max's efforts to suggest opportunities I might like to consider, I've never developed much of a taste for the trappings of wealth so I tend to live fairly quietly — figuratively, that is as well as literally. I buy nice clothes, no economies there. And my apartment is beautifully furnished and equipped — not that you could tell under all the clutter I accumulate. I skip off to New South Wales to catch up with Margaret a couple of times a year, and on the odd occasions that I decide I want something, I just buy it. With the notable exception of Nicholas Hardisty.

It was as I set out on one of my long, solitary journeys to see Margaret that I found myself browsing the shelves in WHSmiths at Manchester airport. I was looking for something to keep me amused between airline meals and the in-flight movies when I came across *that book*. Copies were piled high by the entrance and selling by the cart-load. I admired the rather fetching black and white cover, discreetly adorned by a gray tie, then checked over my shoulder to make sure no one was looking. I wondered what all the fuss could be about and decided there was one way to find out. So I bought it. I brazened it out with the bored-looking spotty teenager on the till, who frankly couldn't have cared less anyway, and stuffed my purchase discreetly inside my hand luggage. And there it stayed until I was safely ensconced in first class, my complementary dry white wine on the table in front of me, and the Qantas steward nowhere in sight. I dragged out my book, and didn't put it down for eight hours.

Apart from enforced breaks to eat and go to the loo — white wine has that effect on me, I find — I read it non-stop from cover to cover. And I knew, I just knew, this was for me. I tingled, clenched and shivered through all the sexy scenes, re-reading most of them for good measure. To make sure I didn't miss anything important. Desperate to continue my fix of BDSM, I managed to buy the sequel at Singapore, and hunted down the third installment in a bookstore at Kingsford Smith Airport in Sydney. I was antisocial for the best part of a week as I claimed jet lag and greedily devoured the rest.

I wanted to try it for myself, I just had to. I wasn't sure how, when, and certainly not why. But I was determined. And I had money, so surely I could do anything I wanted. Couldn't I?

I did my internet research and came to the conclusion that the best way to embark on this latest venture was to join a club. A nice club, where I could be sure of meeting people with similar interests to my own. Then — who knows? In the event, it didn't turn out to be so simple. The Collared and Tied club is perfectly fine as far as my exacting quality standards are concerned, but until I attracted Nicholas Hardisty's attention, no one there, except for Frank perhaps, was the least bit interested in me. Making conversation with other submissives is a non-starter, and up until my evening with Nicholas, my handful of direct experiences with Doms did not go especially well.

As a new submissive, at first I wasn't short of invitations to play. However, despite my enthusiasm for the idea of submission, the theory of it as understood from my forays into erotic literature, I found the requirement to strip on demand, regardless of my audience, more than a little disconcerting. And I've never become comfortable with the prospect of fucking strangers. I did it though, and despite my reservations and inhibitions was not disappointed with the arousing effects of a well-administered spanking.

Then I met Nicholas Hardisty. He was utterly wonderful, and seemed to have a good time too, but he's not in any obvious hurry to repeat it. And after Nicholas, I have no wish to scene with anyone else. So we have stalemate. Or I do.

Despite my wealth, my shopping list was remarkably brief. One thing I could buy, I suppose, is a synthetic voice. Computers can do wonderful things these days, including converting type into speech. I checked out a couple, but they sound to me like a satnav at best, so I don't bother. My lack of speech has never seemed particularly troublesome to me. It just is what it is. The medical term for my condition is aphonia, which in a nutshell means that my larynx and vocal chords don't work. Apparently I contracted a massive viral infection of my throat and chest when I was about eighteen months old which permanently damaged the nerves, affecting how my larynx functions and paralyzing my vocal chords. So that was me silenced for good. I don't recall a time it was ever any different though, and I've always felt I communicated perfectly well by signing. Until recently that is, in my not especially fulfilling forays into sexual fetishism.

My gran understood British Sign Language. Margaret quickly picked it up, so did a few of my friends at school did, and my special tutors. These people helped me by speaking for me when I needed it. Summer's my best friend. We met when she came to Margaret's while her mother was serving four months in prison for persistent shoplifting, and she's fluent at reading my signing. And of course now there's the internet, emails, texting, where I'm on the same level playing field as everyone else. Obviously I can't use a phone to speak to people and it's awkward in shops sometimes, but I manage to buy a lot of stuff online. And traveling can be a challenge. But mostly I get by just fine. There are far worse problems.

Like loving someone who I can't have, for example. Someone such as Nicholas Hardisty.

* * * *

It's been three weeks since I spent that incredible evening with Nicholas Hardisty at the Collared and Tied club, and I've not been back there. I fought tooth and nail, was prepared to endure just about anything he cared to dish out to me just to hang on to my membership, and I find now I've completely lost interest in the place. I thought it was so important, so fundamental to my happiness, my sexual fulfilment — I felt desperate, distraught when he stripped me of it. Now I couldn't care less.

It's because of him. It's because he doesn't want me, and I can't even start to think about wanting anyone else. I have no interest in scening with any other Dom, can't imagine allowing any other Dom to touch me, and I know if I went to the club they might. I might well be invited to join in some scene or other, and my popularity has probably increased because I spent that evening so publicly with Nicholas Hardisty. Others would have noticed, would maybe wonder if I might be worth a closer look. Doms who would never have looked twice at me before might be interested now, and I'd have to turn them down because they're not Nicholas Hardisty. That wouldn't go down well, not for long. Unless you're in an exclusive arrangement, submissives are sort of expected to be available, amenable to all reasonable offers, so to speak. And these days, I'm none of those things. So I stay at home.

Summer hasn't come back yet either, although I've had several texts from her assuring me she's fine. I had an email from Nicholas Hardisty the day after our encounter at the club telling me that Daniel Praed had also vouched for her health and safety when she left him that night, so I suppose she must be okay. It would be good to see for myself though.

I've thrown myself into a frenzy of quilting and designing, done some of my best work in the last couple of weeks—amazing what abject misery and total solitude can do for the creative juices, it would seem. I've not been going out, not even turned the television on for weeks. The nearest I get to the outside world is the odd half hour on my balcony watching the river flowing below me, and only then at night usually.

Am I lonely? No. Well, it's not only loneliness. I'm hiding. I'm licking my wounds and taking stock. And I'm trying to work out where to go from here. Apart from making lovely quilts, there's a whole lot of nothing else I need to do. A whole world of no one needing me at all, of no one relying on me for anything. I may have money, but it doesn't buy happiness. Or love. And it definitely can't buy me Nicholas Hardisty.

I've over forty-million pounds sitting in the bank, and the one thing I would want to buy is not for sale.

Chapter Seven

I can't be bothered to get out of bed, but I suppose I'll have to eventually. It's getting on for three in the afternoon, and I'm slipping into some really bad habits here. If I find myself watching Countdown in my pajamas, it's time to get sorted. Even my precious quilting is losing its appeal. I need someone to talk to, I really do. But Summer's still AWOL. There's nothing else for it, I need Margaret. I can't just ring her up, but I could Skype her. She'll be able to put me on video and read my signing.

Or better still, maybe I could get a flight and go to see her. Yes, that's what I want to do. Time to drag my arse out of bed and get online. Got to buy an airline ticket.

So, it's with some semblance of a sense of purpose that I tug my laptop out from under the settee and plug it into the mains. I fire it up, waiting patiently while the little icons flash and leap about on the screen as the whole carry on lazily hauls its own arse into gear. I'm reminded of the palaver Margaret used to have to go through to get me out of bed on a school day when I was about fourteen. My laptop's hit puberty I think. It's become a stroppy teenager. Next thing it'll be demanding money for hair straighteners and a new bra. Oh well...

I spot the unread email icon flashing on my task bar and open my Outlook. Might as well delete the junk mail while I'm here.

Shit! There's a stack of emails from Nicholas Hardisty. I skim through them, and can see that he's been emailing me for days, and getting no response.

From: Nicholas Hardisty
To: Freya Stone
Date: 20 May 2013
Subject: Are you playing hard to get?

From: Nicholas Hardisty
To: Freya Stone
Date: 21 May 2013
Subject: Playing Hard to get
You've not been to the club for weeks. Frank says you used to come at least twice a week. I repeat – are you avoiding me?

From: Nicholas Hardisty
To: Freya Stone
Date:21 May 2013
Subject: FREYA – respond please

From: Nicholas Hardisty
To: Freya Stone
Date: 22 May 2013
Subject: Bloody hell, Freya!
You're pissing me off, girl. And you know how unpleasant I can get when you piss me off. I want to know if

you're all right. And I want to know why you haven't been to the club. And I want to know NOW.
Nick

It's clear he's not best pleased. I re-read his messages, and I'm puzzled. Why the concern? I mean, it's nice, lovely in fact, but why would he care? Why would he bother talking to Frank about me? Why would he imagine I'd want to avoid him? Christ, just the opposite. I want to throw myself at him and beg him to fuck me, if he can find the time that is.

I pull up his latest email and try to think of a response.

From: Freya Stone
To: Nicholas Hardisty
Date: 23 May 2013
Subject: I'm fine, thanks
Good afternoon, Mr Hardisty
Sorry, I've only just turned my laptop on. I didn't mean to ignore you. I haven't fancied going to the club for a while. If you let me know when you'll next be there, I'll try to make it too.
It would be really nice to see you again.
Freya

From: Nicholas Hardisty
To: Freya Stone
Date: 23 May 2013
Subject: I don't make dates with subs
But I'll keep an eye out for you
Nick

Oh. Oh well. And…Nick? Not Nicholas then. I sit on the edge of my settee staring at the screen and wondering how he got the idea I was trying to make a date with him. I need to set him straight.

From: Freya Stone
To: Nick Hardisty
Date: 23 May 2013
Subject: Dates
Good afternoon again
I didn't mean a date. I just meant that I'll make sure I'm there if you let me know when's convenient for you. Otherwise though, I've no plans to be at the club again for a while.
Best regards
Freya

A bit formal, but I can't help it. He really does get the wrong end of the stick a lot too easily.

From: Nicholas Hardisty
To: Freya Stone
Date: 26 May 2013
Subject: You fucking win!
All right. If your offer still stands, I'm willing to discuss it. But no fee. Absolutely no room for negotiation there.
Meet me for a coffee. We'll talk. Or I'll talk, you'll listen. And write.
Nick
P.S. Email me your mobile number

I win! I fucking win! What's that supposed to mean?

Who cares what it means. He wants to see me. Wants to talk to me. At me, whatever. I email him back my mobile number as requested. No, scratch that, as *instructed*. And I wait.

But I don't wait for long. Within five minutes the ping from my phone tells me a text has arrived. And sure enough, it's from him.

Meet me at Costa, in Kendal town center. Half an hour.

Half an hour! Shit! Still, no point messing about. I quickly punch in my reply.

I'll be there.

In the event, it takes me forty minutes to throw some decent clothes on and scurry down into town to the Costa coffee shop. I know he won't take kindly to me being late. Doms tend to get distinctly shirty about things like that, and I'm already flustered as I rush through the door. At first, I think I might have somehow managed to get here before him as I gaze frantically around and he's not there, only to spot him lounging on an outside table in the alley next to the coffee shop. There are two cups in front of him—looks like he might have ordered for me already. I take a deep breath, hoping to steady myself a bit before facing him again, and I step back outside.

As I approach, he uses his foot to nudge the spare chair at his table out for me to sit on. I nod my thanks and take the seat, earning myself a few more moments respite by gesturing at the spare coffee then at myself, asking if that's for me.

"Yeah. I remembered you like it white, no sugar. That right?"

I nod then take a sip. I replace the cup carefully in its saucer and meet his eyes. Slate gray, icy, piercing. And not at all amused. I'm puzzled—he invited me after all. He didn't have to be here. I swallow nervously, and wait for him to tell me what this is all about. He bides his time, taking a sip of his coffee himself before leaning back in his chair to watch me squirming in front of him. Eventually he speaks.

"So, do you still want to be trained? In the fine and noble art of submission?"

A good question. Do I? Yes, in a manner of speaking, but my parameters have changed. I want him to train me—I want to learn from him, for him. Only him. Is that what he's offering? A long term Dom/sub relationship? I seriously doubt that. But, ever the pragmatist, maybe I just need to take what I can get, accept the limits of what's on offer and live for now. I'm a natural optimist, and I can't help but hope for more later. Maybe I'll end up being disappointed. I accept that possibility, but I have to try.

So I nod. Slowly but definitely. I'm in.

He sits up straighter, leaning in toward me, his gaze holding mine. In that moment he reminds me of my bank manager, the one I used to have to persuade when I was a hard-up student begging for an overdraft at the Nat-West, obviously. Dealing with Max Furrowes and his colleagues at Lloyds Private Bank is a whole different kettle of fish, it goes without saying. Nicholas—Nick—Hardisty is of the Nat-West variety.

"Okay. I'll give you a month then. One month of exclusive, intensive one on one tuition. You'll spend that month with me, at my home. It'll be hard. Very hard. And you'll hurt in places you never even knew you had. You'll have no privacy, no secrets. Your body will be mine for that month, your time, your life, all mine, willingly given up to me." His voice is curt, business-like, formal. My knickers are dampening just listening to him.

"You'll do exactly as I say, however difficult it is, however scared or humiliated you feel. And it will be bloody hard. You'll think I'm brutal at times. You'll be frightened, embarrassed, tired, sore. But I'll thrill you too, delight you. I'll make you feel so fucking good, Freya, you'll think you've gone to heaven. And there'll be no respite, no let up. Once we start, you're mine for the duration, or unless you decide to end it. You once asked me what I'd consider a fair price for training you. Well that's it. That's my price. Whatever I ask, whatever I instruct you to do, you do your level best to deliver. No excuses, no delaying. You just do it. If you decide my price is too high, you can walk away at any time, but if you do decide to walk, that's the training program finished. Over. So, are you up for that, Freya?"

In truth, I'm his forever, if he did but know it. I hadn't expected the one month twenty-four-seven arrangement, but I don't object to that. In theory at least I know what's involved, although I can only imagine how some of it could make me feel. Degraded? Powerless? Helpless? Delirious? Those emotional aspects rather than the physical pain are the issues which concern me, but they come with the territory. Don't they? I'm turning all this over in my head, although I know already, knew from the outset, that I'd accept whatever terms he put before me.

He leans in again. "For a natural submissive—and, honey, after the evening we spent together, I do believe you are a natural—submission to a Dom you trust is intensely satisfying. Liberating." Now his tone has become gentler. Lower, more seductive. "You hand over control, and in exchange can expect all your sensual, emotional and physical needs to be met. I'm offering to show you that, to take you there if that's what you want. If you'll trust me, if you'll let me take care of you as you explore what's deep within you, and make your journey. So, will you trust me, little Freya?"

Put like that...

I nod. Yes, of course I'll trust him, I always did. So, I'm still in.

He smiles, his gray eyes now softer, warming as he regards me, raking my body as he did that evening at the club, and I suspect he's mentally stripping my clothes away. Not that I mind overly much—nudity is a big part of this deal, I do know that. And talking of which, his specific instructions grab my attention, including taking nakedness to a whole new level for me.

"Right, here's how it's going to happen. You'll spend the month at my home, and during that time we'll be together twenty-four-seven. You'll live with me, eat with me, sleep with me and your body will be available for training at any time. Don't worry about food, accommodation, any of that. You'll be very well cared for, very comfortable indeed. Except for when I'm hurting you, obviously."

I nod my understanding. Obviously.

He continues. "I already have all the equipment we'll need, but of course if you have any favorite toys or implements please feel free to bring those too. I have to go away on business from tomorrow for a few weeks, so we won't start our program for another six weeks, but then it'll be full on, until the month's up. Neither of us will have any other outside commitments, is that clear? You need to clear your diary for the entire month and I'll do the same—no distractions, no interruptions."

Wow—he does mean 'full on'. And what diary? What commitments? I was thinking about going to Australia, but I can be back in time for this. A whole lot of nothing is what my long-term diary consists of. I just nod, no problem there as far as I can see.

"Right, I'm glad that's clear then. And you'll have some work to do in the six weeks between now and when we start. To start with, I like my subs naked. Properly naked. So I want you to make sure all your body hair is removed. And I mean all. I prefer you to be waxed rather than shave—lasts longer and it's a better job. Have you ever had a full Brazilian wax?" He pauses, lifts an eyebrow as he waits for my response.

I gulp, shake my head nervously. Now this I don't like the sound of. I just know this'll hurt. He reads my mind, as ever.

"Coward—I have far more…excruciating treatments planned for you. And I won't be offering pain relief. This place will though…" He shoves a business card across the table at me.

I pick it up, glance at it—*Pretty Things Beauty Parlour*.

"These guys can sort you out, unless there's somewhere else you know of and prefer to use?"

I shake my head, slipping the card into my bag for later.

"Okay. You can charge any expenses like this to me. I don't expect you to pay."

I shrug, least of my worries. And I'll pay extra for the pain relief.

"I also want you to have a full medical check-up. The medic retained by the Collared and Tied club can do it, she knows what sort of information I'll be needing. I want to know about any underlying health conditions, anything at all that might affect your fitness to endure the demands of what I intend to do to you. With you. Anything I should watch out for, or need to take into account..." I dive for my bag. There's something I need to ask, need to tell him before the doctor does. He pauses, waits for me as I fish around in my bag. I pull out my Samsung Galaxy phone, glad I remembered to shove it in there as I was dashing out of my apartment, and note his silent nod of approval as I start to write.

Does diabetes count?

I pass the note to him. He glances at it, then at me.
"Oh yes, I'm sure it does. Are you on medication? Do you need any treatment? Are you likely to go into a diabetic coma as soon as I wave a whip at you?"
I take my notepad back, and start writing again.

No, none of that. I don't take any medicine. Not yet. But I have to eat very carefully. Healthy food like fruit and vegetables, wholemeal bread. Pasta. Low fat, low salt. And no sugar. Absolutely no sugar – that's very important. Will that be OK, my diet I mean?

Again he reads, and again he glances sharply back at me. "The diet's fine. We'll manage that no problem." He points to my screen. "What do you mean, 'yet'?"
More typing and I pass the phone back to him.

I'll probably need to take medication eventually, but I can control my blood sugar fairly well so far by eating properly. I have done for years.

He nods, seemingly satisfied for now. "Make sure the medic knows about your diabetes. I'll expect to see it mentioned in the report, and I'll want to get the all clear. And I want you to sort out contraception too. We'll use condoms some of the time, but I don't want any accidents coming back to haunt either of us later."

Again I reach for my phone.

I'm on the Pill already — is that OK?

"Yes, that's fine. Again, I want to see it confirmed in the medical report. And I'll be wanting blood tests for HIV, hepatitis, STD's, the usual. The doctor will know. I'll supply you with the same information, naturally."

Naturally.

"There'll be more details I'll need you to know and I'll let you have those in due course, exact dates, times, location, that sort of thing. And I may have more instructions for you. I'll text you, as you seem good at ignoring my emails. If — when — you get any message from me I expect you to acknowledge it immediately, and respond as appropriate. Is that clear?"

I nod, but that's not enough apparently.

"Just so there's no doubt, I need you to understand that although we don't get into it properly for another six weeks, you and I have an agreement from now on. I expect you to obey my instructions, and assume the proper attitude of respect. There will be breaches, you're learning, and to help you to learn, I'll correct any lapses incurred during this next six weeks at the start of our intensive month. You *will* be disciplined if required, and that discipline will be physical. The severity of any punishment will obviously depend on the nature and extent of your misdemeanors. Do you accept that? Will you accept punishment and learn from it?"

So, here it is, the nub of our relationship. This is what a Dom/sub agreement hinges on. And once I accept this, once I agree to his terms, from then on I acknowledge his authority over me, and his right to punish me. I allowed him that right once, and he delivered a punishment beating I'll never, ever forget. Maybe I'll never attract anything of that severity again, but I can't be sure. But this is not about being sure. This is about trust—trusting my Dom and trusting myself. I nod, and by way of additional emphasis offer him my hand to shake. He takes it, and our deal is sealed.

He smiles at me again. "Well, Miss Stone, we're going to have an interesting time together. I'm looking forward to it. Now, you live near here I believe…?"

I nod, wondering how he knows where I live, but I don't have time to ask him before he continues. "If you've finished your coffee, we'll go to your apartment now, because, with your agreement obviously, I intend to fuck you. And they don't take kindly to that sort of thing here in Costa. Upsets the other customers and leaves a sticky mess on the tables. But first, there's the matter of you being ten minutes late meeting me here. We'll need to deal with that. Shall we go?"

He stands, as I do, and he gestures for me to precede him back onto the main pavement. I do as I'm told. Might as well start as I mean to go on.

Chapter Eight

The ten minute walk along the River Kent, back to my apartment block, passes in silence. Only to be expected I suppose, he's said all he needs to say for now. And I have the matter of my ten minutes of tardiness to contemplate, which has without doubt earned me some form of retribution.

We reach my building, and I lead the way inside, nodding to the concierge as we pass through the lobby and over to the lift. I live on the top floor, the fifth — no really high rise stuff here in the traditional heartland of the Lake District. Tourists don't go for that sort of thing. But even given the planning constraints of the neighborhood — which I don't think of as detracting at all from my environment — I simply love it here. I chose to come back here when I could have stayed in Australia, or gone anywhere in the world. This is home. A spacious, modern apartment with access to a communal swimming pool and spa, and a top class cleaning and maintenance service obviously adds to the attractions. But essentially it was location that drew me. And that's what holds me here. I love to sit on my balcony just watching the world go by. In one direction I can watch the river tumbling and meandering away toward the sea, and if I turn my head I can look upstream to the bustling town center. And if I lift my gaze over the rooftops I can see the rolling hills of the south Lakes in every direction. Superb. Breathtaking in the spring and summer, but absolutely stunning in the autumn and the winter, this easy, undulating landscape, so rich in color and so gentle on the eye.

I've lived here for four years now, and I suppose I've become accustomed to it. I don't see the luxury any more certainly, I just see my home. And as Summer is the only visitor I tend to have here, the reactions of others are something of a novelty. And that's why Nick Hardisty's long, low whistle as I unlock the door leading into my hallway comes as a surprise. He follows me inside, turning through three hundred and sixty degrees as he surveys my domain.

"You didn't buy this place with Tesco Clubcard points... Your Lottery winnings again?"

I nod as he strolls across my hallway and into my open plan living area. I'm keenly aware of the untidy clutter around the room, but my biggest concern is how to field the questions he's sure to ask me about my lottery win. People always do. They always want to know how much I won. What I bought. What I'm planning to buy next. For many, their curiosity satisfied, it ends there. But for some this is the point when they start to make their suggestions. This is when they sound me out for possible investments in their pet projects or donations to their charities. This is the begging letter stage, and it makes me cringe. Worse still, this is sometimes the point when the acquisitive and the manipulative and the just plain greedy start to cultivate my friendship. This is where they start fawning over me, pretending to like me when really it's the prospect of exploiting my generosity that's the real attraction.

I have no reason to assume that's Nick Hardisty's motivation for being here. He's no mercenary. If he was, he'd already be twenty-five thousand pounds richer, and I'd be thinking I'd gotten myself a decent bargain. And more importantly, I'd know exactly where I stood with him. Our relationship would be clear. Now, I'm off balance, uncertain. And totally confused by his refusal to accept my money whilst still agreeing to provide me with the service I want. And it's that confusion, that uncertainty, coupled with my innately private nature, that drives me to want to conceal the details of my financial affairs from him now. Keeping myself to myself is the habit of a lifetime, and I won't be changing any time soon.

Not that he seems especially interested. He glances at me, a half smile on his gorgeous lips as he strolls to the window to check out my view. Turning back to me, his hip perched on the window ledge, he gestures to the jumbled luxury surrounding us. "So, you bought this place then? And a car? You have good taste, Freya, in cars and property. This place is lovely." He pauses as something catches his eye, and leans sideways to extract a rather beautiful silk scarf from behind a radiator, holds it out to me.

"Yours, I assume?"

I nod and take the scarf, one of my favorites, I'd been wondering where it had gotten to.

"Take care of that—I think it may come in useful soon."

I'm happily contemplating the implications of that prospect as he continues. "Do you have a job, Freya?"

I was hoping he wouldn't ask me anything along those lines. I shake my head slowly, and he shrugs. "So what do you do for money then? Just live off the rest? You're only young, what did you say when we were at the club? Twenty-three?"

I nod.

"Even a few hundred thousand in the bank won't keep you in silk scarves forever, not living in a place like this and with your taste in cars. And clothes. What'll you do when the money runs out?"

I can't suppress a smile. He actually thinks I'm extravagant. Me? But now's the time to set his assumptions straight if I'm going to. Now's the time to agree that a few hundred thousand would indeed be easy to fritter away. But at my present rate of expenditure it would actually take me well over four hundred years to exhaust my funds, and that's only if Max Furrowes' grasp of prudent investment were to evaporate this very instant. As it is, my capital actually increases by around half a million a year, and all I have to do for that is sign whatever papers Max puts in front of me at our half yearly meetings. There's no immediate danger of destitution. I won't be forced to go job-hunting any time this century. Or the next.

But I don't say any of that. Instead I let it be, leave his assumption unchallenged. And Nick Hardisty just shrugs, dismissing my apparently woeful lack of financial planning as none of his business no doubt, as he crouches to retrieve the collected works of William Wordsworth and an upturned mug from under my coffee table.

Not normally bothered by the clutter, I find myself viewing the chaos of my living room through his eyes. And I'm embarrassed by it. I just dropped everything and rushed out as soon as I got his text. It never occurred to me he'd come back here with me, and even if it had, I'm not the tidy sort. I rarely, if ever, bother to clear up so my quilting stuff is strewn everywhere, my sewing machine still perched on the dining table at one end of the room. Scraps of fabric and cardboard cut-out templates are scattered around all adjacent surfaces. My pretty glass-headed pins are piled up on the corner of my coffee table, and he stoops to pick one up as he passes, still strolling casually around my home.

"For self defense?" His head dipped, he looks at me under his raised eyebrows.

I shrug, nervous suddenly. And self-conscious. This might be my home turf, but his approval matters to me, a lot more than I ever imagined it might. I'm wealthy—clearly much, much wealthier than he imagines, but I did nothing of note to earn it. I just bought the winning ticket and managed not to lose the bloody thing before the draw. What if he doesn't approve of gambling? What if he thinks I'm just some spoiled rich kid? Worse still, what if he decides after all that he fancies a share of my money and that's the only reason he's bothering with me?

"You'll bring none of this with you. Leave your cashcards, your fancy apartment, leave the lot behind you. You won't need any money."

I'm already pretty sure his interest in me is not financial given his attitude toward my offer of payment, but this remark dispels it entirely. He continues, "You'll need to come in your car I suppose, and bring a few clothes, but that's it. Most of the time you won't be wearing anything in any case. It's to be just you and me. Understood?"

Once more I nod, grateful that the gesture meaning 'yes' is universally understood. I suspect I'll be using it a whole lot more as my association with Nick Hardisty develops.

He wanders across the room to my dining table, the paraphernalia of quilting scattered across the surface, seemingly aimlessly, but I know better than to imagine that. He idly picks up a small square made up of fabrics carefully cut and pieced together to form a picture of a vixen and fox cub, part of a much larger quilt I'm making, my contribution to an exhibition next year to celebrate the ten year anniversary of the ban on fox hunting. He glances back at me.

"This is pretty. What's it going to be?"

I step forward, reaching around him to pull out a quilt I completed a few weeks ago, this one a Roman-style mosaic. I show that to him, and reach around him once more, this time to pick up the rolled up sheet of flipchart paper I used to sketch out and measure the design I made for the vixen piece. I show him the overall pattern, a collection of scenes depicting the fox in its natural habitat, and point to where the piece he has in his hands will fit eventually. Several other squares, already completed, are piled up on the table, and I lay those out in their final intended sequence to show how it will all work together.

To his credit, he does seem genuinely interested, and impressed with my work. As indeed he should be—I am extremely good at this. It's a bit of a niche hobby, but highly skilled. A completed quilt can be extremely intricate, requiring hundreds, probably thousands of small pieces of fabric all carefully measured, cut to size, and sewn together perfectly. The execution is difficult enough, but I also design my own stuff, and some of my designs even sell.

"This looks like a very exact science, Miss Stone. Do you have to measure and cut each piece individually?" The bland question seems innocent enough.

I nod, indicating with my head the clear plastic grid square I use and the eighteen inch ruler with a metal edge for accurate scalpel and wheel cutting. He smiles softly as he picks up the ruler, tensing it in his hands as he watches me. And the blood drains from my face as, too late, I realize his intent.

"Ten minutes, wasn't it, Miss Stone? I think that calls for ten strokes, and this will do very nicely. Are you wearing underwear?"

My mouth is dry as I nod.

"I thought so. Quite decent and proper. Remove it please. Then if you'd be so kind as to clear a space among your work, lift your skirt up above your waist, and bend over the table, that would be much appreciated." His bombshell dropped, his instructions issued, he leans back, his hips casually hitched on the edge of my table as he waits for me to comply.

My hands are shaking as I hook my thumbs in the elastic at the front of my panties and draw them down. I step out of them then place the white lacy scrap in his outstretched palm. He dangles the delicate concoction from his forefinger, glancing at my pants, then at me. "Very pretty, Miss Stone. Very feminine. They suit you. Please make sure you bring plenty more like this when you come to stay. And I promise you'll have some even prettier stripes across your bum in a few minutes. The table, please?"

He watches, unmoving, as I arrange my completed quilt squares back into a neat and tidy pile then place them carefully next to the sewing machine at one end of the table. I collect up my other bits and pieces— fabrics, cardboard shapes, pins, cotton reels, scissors, cutting wheel, and place them close to the sewing machine too, leaving half the table empty and clear. Ample space for me to stretch out across the table top and bare my bottom for his punishment.

He evidently thinks so too. He nods and stands, a sharp tilt of his head indicating that I should assume the position. The memory of the discipline he meted out to me at the club is still fresh in my mind, so I'm in no real hurry to do this. This was not what I expected when I rushed out of here less than an hour ago to run down to Costa to meet him, and I didn't dawdle then. I got there as quickly as I could, half an hour just wasn't enough time. This is really not fair…

With a growing sense of injustice I scowl briefly over my shoulder at Nick Hardisty as I start to gather my skirt, bunching it in my hands ready to raise it above my waist.

"You have something to say, Miss Stone?" His tone is formal and clipped, stern.

I drop the fabric, my long, loose skirt once more swishing safely around my calves as I glance back at him. He steps forward, the ruler still in his hand as he picks up a pencil from my little pile of stuff by my sewing machine and passes it to me. I glance around among the chaos for something to write on, spotting a few small pieces of paper that I'd been using as templates for shape cutting. I pull one toward me and start writing.

I got there as fast as I could. You didn't give me enough time.

And, an afterthought—

I'm sorry I was late. Truly.

He reads my note, then locks his glacial gaze on me once more. "You should have said you needed longer. We could have arranged to meet later. Then you could have arrived on time." He steps forward, taking my chin between his thumb and forefinger, he holds my gaze truly captive. "If I instruct you to do something that you believe you can't do, you must tell me, re-negotiate, explain. Otherwise you'll fail to obey, and you'll be punished. Like now. Do you understand what you need to do to avoid this situation arising again in the future, Miss Stone?"

I nod, blinking back my own tears of frustration that I let this happen. I was so eager to see him again, so pleased to hear from him, I just never considered, never thought...

"But still you feel I'm being unjust?"

I start to shake my head, but his fingers on my chin hold me still. "Don't lie to me, Miss Stone. If you feel I'm being too hard on you, you can say so. We'll talk about it. You won't learn from a punishment you feel is unwarranted. And that's what a punishment is for, to help you to learn the right things to do, the correct attitude, the acceptable way to behave. So, what do *you* think would be fair?"

Just fuck me, nicely, I'd settle for that.

Not happening, at least, not until he's dealt with my disobedience. I reach for the pencil again, and write another note.

I'll accept whatever you think is right. I'm sorry, I realize I should have said I needed more time.

I pass my note back, and wait.

His tone is still hard, stern, but his eyes less chilled now. He watches me for a few seconds, considering, then, "Good answer, Miss Stone. You're learning. You've earned ten strokes, but I think five will get my message across. This time. Fair?"

I smile, nod. He steps back, gesturing with his free hand toward the table. "Right, let's get this done then. Raise your skirt and bend over the table please."

This time I do as I'm asked. Whilst not exactly enthusiastic, I manage to comply with considerably less reluctance than a few minutes ago. Five strokes, I can handle that. It'll be over in no time. Won't it? And then...

I bunch my skirt in my hands again and turn to face the table. I lean across it, instinctively stretching my arms out in front of me, gripping the opposite edge with my fingers. I hear his footsteps as he positions himself behind me.

"I'm sure you'll be fine, only five strokes, Miss Stone. But just in case, if you need a safe signal, you do two sharp slaps on the table top, like this." He leans over me, slaps his palm twice on the table to demonstrate. "That'll stop me, if you need to. Do you understand?"

I nod, thankful and encouraged that, even now, even when it's just five strokes and we both know I can cope with that, he still gives me safe signals to protect myself. I was right about Nick Hardisty, I *will* be well cared for, with him.

Five strokes, hard ones to be sure, but only five. The first has my breath hissing out sharply. *Christ, that hurts.* Even though I know what to expect now, the next is no better, and I gasp, my knuckles whitening as my death-grip on the edge of my table tightens. My eyes are watering on the third—the fourth and fifth draw my first sobs. Then it's done, over almost before it's begun.

Nick Hardisty places the ruler flat on the table beside my face. I start to rise, but his hand on the small of my back keeps me pinned there.

"Don't move just yet. Stay there."

He walks away, crosses my living area in the direction of what I suppose he must have worked out are the bedrooms and my bathroom. Sure enough, he's back a few moments later with a damp flannel and a tub of Sudocrem. It's usually sold for nappy rash, but I've found it really soothing when dealing with the aftermath of a decent spanking, though I usually have to apply it myself. Not this time though. Nick Hardisty smoothes the cream across my bottom, gently rubbing it in. I manage not to squirm too much, especially as discomfort changes quickly to arousal as he pays more attention than perhaps strictly necessary to the furrow between my buttocks. I part my legs instinctively as his fingers slide lower. He's exploring now, moving on to the next chapter, parting my labia to dip one fingertip into my moist and ready entrance.

"Where's your bedroom, Miss Stone?"

His mouth is beside my ear, and I feel his breathe on the sensitive spot just behind it as he whispers the words. He withdraws his wonderful, skilled fingers from my body, and again, I start to push myself up. This time his hands are there to help me, and I find myself standing, then he turns me in his arms, kisses me briefly. "The bedroom? Or do I fuck you here on your table?"

I point in the general direction, and he takes my right hand in his left, using the other hand to gesture me to lead the way. I do, hoping I didn't leave the place in too much of a tip this morning. Would he spank me for my slovenly domestic habits too, I wonder? Or worse?

Apparently not. Nick doesn't seem to notice the tangled sheets and cluttered floor as he picks me up in the doorway of my bedroom and tumbles me onto the bed under the window. He follows me onto the bed, rolling me under him for a long, dragging kiss. He plunges his tongue deep, tangling with mine as he tastes and explores, his fingers deftly unfastening the buttons down the front of my blouse. I help by shrugging out of the blouse and tossing it onto the floor to join the rest of next week's washing.

He makes short work of my bra, which soon adds to the pile beside the bed as he releases my mouth at last. But only to work his way down, nibbling his way over my jaw and neck, across my shoulder and down to my elbow, then up again to trace the underside of my breast before opening his lips around my erect nipple. He sucks on it, lightly at first, then more firmly. I remember the intensity of sensation when we scened in the dungeon, the agony and the exquisite ecstasy of the nipple clamps he used to arouse and entice me, and in my mind I'm there again. I tilt my head back as I arch up to offer more of myself, to beg him for more.

He continues to suckle, hard and greedy, as he unfastens his own shirt and flings it aside. Then he takes hold of my waist and rolls onto his back, pulling me around to land on top of him. He hooks his thumbs in the waistband of my skirt and eases it down over my hips. I wince slightly as it scrapes over my bottom, but the sensation is one of pleasant soreness. He knows, and his palm is there, caressing my tender buttocks as he continues to tease and nip at my breasts. He alternates his attention from one to the other as I comb my fingers through his hair. My legs are open, straddling him, and he abandons my smarting bum to once more probe my entrance, testing my wetness, my readiness.

He moves again, this time to roll me onto my back. He thrusts his finger deep into me, and I gasp my approval, squeezing down instinctively.

"Ah, baby, that's so sweet. Sweet and hot and tight." His voice is a low, sexy murmur as he's once again on the move, heading farther south.

He stops briefly to dip his tongue into my navel before continuing down, past my now outlawed pubic hair to position himself between my legs. He stops, takes his time to explore with his eyes, using both hands now to open my labia, exposing my sensitive inner lips. He gently opens and closes me, licking his own lips as he carefully picks his spot. Then he lowers his head to flick the tip of my clit with his tongue before he slowly, deliberately, circles it. He licks the sensitive, engorged bud, just lightly at first, then pressing more heavily with his tongue as I arch and squirm under him. All the time his hands are there, holding me open, exposed and perfectly positioned for his attentions.

My orgasm is on me in moments, bubbling up swiftly, an avalanche of tingling sensation which quickly engulfs me, sizzling, connecting every nerve ending with my throbbing, empty core. I'm shuddering, my awareness now of everything in the room narrowed and focused on this man, this Dom, and what he's doing to me with his wicked, knowing tongue. And I want him inside me. Now. Any way he likes. But it has to be now!

As ever, he knows. Kneeling, he unbuttons his jeans and slides the zip down. In moments they too have joined the pile on the floor, along with his boxer shorts. He has a condom foil packet in his hand, retrieved from his jeans pocket before he dumped them, and he snaps that open with his teeth. He's kneeling between my legs, and he offers me the condom to unroll over him. I take it, my fingers only shaking very slightly as I do the honors. Fully sheathed, he leans forward, stretching out to lie over me, his weight supported on his elbows as he looks down at me, spread out under him, ready, waiting, willing and eager. He smiles, his gaze warm, sexy as he lowers his head to brush my lips with his at the same instant he thrusts into me.

He swallows my breathy gasp, and the ones that follow as he continues to thrust, long and deep, but slow. He seems to be relishing this, drawing out every sensation as I convulse under him, around him. My fingers are digging into his shoulders as I grab him and hang on as he picks up the pace. His thrusts are faster now, harder. Instinctively I lift my legs and wrap them around his waist, the sharper angle increasing the penetration. The head of his cock nudges my cervix with each stroke, and it's fabulous. Absolutely wonderful. My inner muscles take on a life of their own as they squeeze him hard, the movements involuntary now as my arousal grows and peaks. Within moments I'm coming once more, my breath ragged as I'm carried along on yet another amazing wave of mind-blowing sensation. His mouth is now on my neck, nuzzling, nipping me as his own climax builds and explodes. His low curse is muffled against my shoulder an instant before the hot wash of semen fills the condom. He plunges once more, deep inside me, holds that position for long seconds to savor his own release.

My eyes are closed as I wait for the world to right itself once more. I feel him relax, the tension of orgasm dissipating quickly as he drops another swift kiss on my lips.

"Christ, girl, when you decide to expand your horizons, you do it right. That was fucking wonderful."

My thoughts exactly, but the best I can manage is a smile before he rolls over and I find myself on top once more. He quickly lifts me, breaking our connection to dispose of the condom which he knots and tosses into a waste bin beside my bed, full of tissues and other girlie rubbish. I really must tidy up…

He settles me back alongside him, half across his chest and half snuggled in to his side. He's idly stroking my back, and he's silent. Thinking? Planning?

For once I've been doing a bit of planning of my own. He's instructed me to make and keep various appointments in preparation for our intensive month of my training, and I will. It's not as simple as he thinks though. I can't just phone up the beauty salon and arrange a time to show up for my Brazilian wax treatment. Nor can I phone to arrange the medical checks he's insisting on. Unless Summer turns up sometime soon, I'll be reduced to actually going along to these places and doing the best I can to make myself understood over the counter. A notebook or my phone usually does the trick of course, but it's cumbersome. If he'll help, make the calls perhaps, that will make a big difference to me. And I need to ask him soon, before he disappears on his business trip.

And there's another thing now. I was intending to visit Margaret in Australia. I still am, I hope, and I've time to make the trip in the six weeks he's allowed me between now and the start of my training. But I'm not sure of the rules. Do I need his permission? He did say that our 'arrangement' starts now, so maybe…?

"What's going on in your head, girl? I can hear the cogs whirring from here." His voice is soft and low, warm, not the Dom tone.

I lean up on my elbow to look him in the face, wondering where my iPad might be in all this chaos. He's in a good mood so now might be a good time to ask him for help. I put up a hand, indicating that he should wait, and I scramble off the bed. I rummage around on my dressing table, find my tablet and press the 'on' switch. It's fired up and ready by the time I clamber back alongside him, and he casually loops his arm across my shoulders to pull me back in.

I need to make some appointments, the salon, the doctor. But I can't use the phone. Would you mind ringing them for me?

He glances at my screen. "Shit, of course. I should have thought. Sorry. Yes, I'll do it. I'll text you with the dates and times."

I start typing again.

I was planning a trip, to see my family. I'd be back in time for the training, definitely. Is it OK for me to go? You said we'd wait six weeks. I'd do the doctor thing and the waxing before I go if you arrange appointments for as soon as possible.

He reads the note, and glances back at me. "Your family don't live near here then?"

Sydney. New South Wales.

He whistles. "Well that's not exactly just round the corner." He pauses, thinking, then, "When do you leave?"

Ah, no suggestion then that I might not be allowed to go. I'm relieved. I wouldn't have been happy about that, but I would have obeyed him.

I haven't booked a flight yet.

"I see. Well, as long as you're back in time to start our arrangement in six weeks, and as long as you respond when I text you, I don't mind what you get up to in the meantime or where you go. Within reason. You need to plan your trip so I'll sort out your appointments for some time in the next day or so, maybe call in some favors to get it sorted for you. And I'll confirm the date I want you to show up at my home. Will that do?"

I smile, nodding. He really can be very reasonable when he wants to be.

* * * *

"So, did your maid not turn in this week then?" Dressed now in just his jeans, zipped up but still unbuttoned — very sexy — Nick is idly strolling around the chaos which is my living room-come-dining area, idly picking up magazines, empty mugs, discarded junk-mail, books, bits of fabric, half-finished quilting projects. He looks curiously at each item he selects then replaces it exactly as he found it. He catches my gaze, holds it, waits for my answer.

I manage to curtail my drooling at his impressive pectorals and six pack sufficiently to shake my head, shrug. I know I'm untidy, this place is a tip. But I do know where everything is, truly I do. More or less. And in a way he's right about my maid deserting me. Summer usually tidies up, but she's not been around for weeks. Not that I want her to do my housework, but she sort of sneaks up on me.

She often stays here when the din and aggravation at her mother's little house in Barrow gets too much. She has two younger sisters, and an older brother who is serving with the army in Afghanistan. Her mother tends to have what would probably be generously described as a somewhat chaotic lifestyle. She's been known to swan off without warning, leaving Summer to care for the younger ones. It can get pretty manic there, and Summer tells me she hates all the messiness and din. It's true she's neat to the point of compulsiveness, but her aversion to going home is so deep-rooted I suspect there's more to it than just untidiness.

Whatever, Summer definitely appreciates peace and quiet, and order, so she just turns up with a couple of bags and takes up residence in my spare room. We get along fine, and I may be messy, but at least I'm quiet. And she makes it her business to restore order.

She usually waits until my back's turned, when I'm in bed or out shopping or at the Collared and Tied, then she strikes. She tidies and sorts and puts away. She waves a duster around and digs my normally relatively untroubled hoover out from the utility room off my kitchen, where it hides behind the equally untroubled ironing board, and trundles it around the place. I don't like these domestic commando raids much, but at least I know what to expect from her. It takes me weeks to find all my stuff again, and I sort of put up with the meticulous neatness because she's my friend and it's how she likes things. So the system works. I occasionally flirt with the notion of hiring someone to come in a couple of times a week, keep on top of things a bit better, but Summer always manages to talk me out of it. I'm *her* project. By the less than impressed look on Nick Hardisty's face I maybe should be re-visiting that notion.

I reach into the pocket of my short kimono-style wrap for my phone and tap out a short, apologetic message.

I'm sorry. I'm not very tidy I'm afraid. I won't mess your place up though.

He reads my words and glances up at me sardonically, strolling over to me to accept the mug of coffee I've just made him. My kitchen is clean and tidy, I do at least insist on that.

"Oh, I expect you will, Miss Stone. And if your messiness gets too much, I'll have to correct you." He smiles, leaning around me to pat my bottom, then continues to lift the short robe and caress my naked my buttocks suggestively.

I shudder in delighted anticipation at the intimacy of the gesture, the promise of delightfully playful spankings to come. Edging me backwards toward the sofa in the center of the room, Nick places his mug carefully in the space beside a pile of quilting magazines balanced precariously on an antique side table before using his other hand, now free, to lift my hair from my neck. He leans in to nuzzle, sending exquisite little shivers down my spine.

"You may not be a domestic goddess, Freya, but you have other fine qualities. I intend to explore them with you. Thoroughly." He continues his sensual assault, his mouth covering my own, his tongue probing and exploring and drawing mine into an erotic dance.

I reach up, clasping my hands behind his neck and hang on as he lifts me to perch on the back of the sofa. Not breaking the kiss, he unravels the loosely tied belt of my kimono and continues his exploration.

"I could fuck you all night. Would you like that, little sub?" His voice is low, seductive, full of sensual promise, the words dropped lightly into my ear.

I'm melting at the prospect of returning to bed with him. If we get that far. I gasp as two slick fingers slide easily into me, his swift and sure thrusts quickly bringing me back to the brink of orgasm. Then he slows this movements to hold me there, suspended on the edge of ecstasy, tingling with anticipation.

"Unless you have other plans. Do you have any plans for tonight, Freya?"

What? Plans? Nothing long-term. I can't think much past the next few minutes. Seconds even. I wriggle, clenching and writhing against him, and he chuckles as he takes pity on me. A couple of more sharp thrusts, a third finger inside me and the heel of his hand expertly angled to rub my clit, and I'm gone. The delicious, beguiling, absorbing waves of intense pleasure engulf me once more and I simply hang on to him and let it wash over me. My arms are still draped around his neck and his arm around my waist holds me in place as the impact of my release scrambles any sense of balance I might have laid claim to.

"So, do you?" His voice is soft and low.

I look up at him in puzzlement as my senses slowly return to something resembling normal. He catches my frown of confusion.

"Do you have plans for tonight?" he clarifies, helpfully.

I shake my head.

"So, shall we go out somewhere then?" He pauses, then, "Would you let me drive your car, Freya?"

My car? I've been known to let Summer borrow it occasionally, but no one else. No one except Nick Hardisty, it now seems. I find myself nodding.

"Get dressed then." He drops another quick kiss on the top of my head and scoops up his shirt from the back of a chair. I'm still gazing at him, perplexed, as he reaches up to disentangle my hands from around his neck. Then, his hands on my shoulders, he gently turns me and shoves me in the direction of my bedroom again. Alone. "Clothes, Freya. Now."

And I obey, of course.

* * * *

Dressed in jeans and a loose T-shirt, my hair brushed and tamed marginally, now pulled back into a casual pony tail, I settle a little uncertainly in the passenger seat of my Vanquish. Apart from when I bought it, and the Aston Martin dealer insisted on demonstrating all the fine features laid on for my ultimate motoring pleasure, I've never sat in this seat. Nick Hardisty certainly has a unique effect on me, on many levels.

He experiences no such qualms, relaxing easily into the driver's seat, using the electronic controls to shift and adjust his position exactly to his liking, and repeating the exercise with the mirrors and black leather steering wheel. He nods approvingly at the soft beige leather interior upholstery, casually enquiring as to how many cows died to provide the materials. I shrug, honestly never having considered that, but I do have some qualms about the carbon emissions. I know the Vanquish is somewhat on the high side, and I firmly quashed that objection when buying it. Still, the knowledge sits uneasily with my stance on the otherwise high moral ground on all matters relating to sustainability and renewable energy.

Nick easily works out how to use the launch control button and the brake to start the engine, his knowing smile warm as my gas-guzzling guilty pleasure roars into life. The sound fills the underground parking area as he slowly reverses out of my personal bay and heads for the automatic door.

"Let's go find us a lake, shall we?" He glances at me as the roller shutter glides smoothly up to let us exit the car park.

I nod, happy to let him decide. Even so, I assume we're headed for Windermere, the closest lake to us. It's very much a commercial, touristy sort of place, but at this time in the early evening it will probably not be too crowded.

I'm surprised when instead he takes the road leading to Barrow, then turns off to head toward the coast. I guess he's just enjoying the ride as my prized Vanquish purrs easily along the dual carriageway at a steady, almost-silent sixty miles an hour. It could easily do double that, but Nick seems to be taking speed limits seriously. Which is more than I do, sadly, hence my current crop of six points on my driving license and one never-to-be recovered afternoon spent reflecting upon the error of my ways on one of those stern speed awareness courses.

We leave the dual carriageway to hum along the fast but winding road toward the west coast, and my car handles it all quite beautifully. According to the literature, which I studied minutely before I splashed out and bought the car, whilst not especially built to stun on the track, the Vanquish is superb on the road. Just heavy enough to grip and feel secure, light enough to handle at the slightest touch. And as I'm not exactly build like a scaffolder, that matters to me. I like to feel safe while I'm taking my risks, which is sort of why I fixed my attention on this gorgeous man beside me in the first place. I relax, at ease with him and proud of my car. It's not practical, the tiny seats in the back hardly qualify and there's not a lot of luggage space. But I love it, and apparently that makes two of us as Nick continues to put her through her paces.

The miles slide past us as Nick obviously enjoys zipping along the coast road, heading north. He turns off after half an hour or so, and I realize we must be heading for Wastwater. I'm pleased. Not at all commercial, Wastwater is my favorite lake. Dark and brooding, deep, cold, mysterious, I just love the atmosphere here. The secrets and the barely concealed menace, thinly veiled behind a veneer of calm. In the still evening, the unruffled surface of the vast lake comes into view, just the southernmost fingers of it at first, then more as we turn to drive sedately along the narrow road skirting the western shore. Nick has to frequently slow down or stop to avoid suicidal sheep sauntering across the road, and after a few minutes he pulls over into one of the many lay bys provided to cater for the hosts of walkers and tourists who arrive here in droves. Earlier in the day these would be jam-packed by cars abandoned by hikers, campers, fell walkers, but at this time all those hardy souls have left and we have the parking areas all to ourselves. And the lake.

We get out, and Nick doesn't even try to lock the car. No need, it locks itself with a distinct and efficient clunk as we walk away. Instead he holds out his hand to me, and I take it without thinking. Together, our fingers linked, we stroll down to the pebbly lakeside to gaze across at the opposite shore. It's even wilder over there, no road, just a steeply rising fell, layered in various shades of gray, brown and green as the rocks give way to shale, then bracken, then more luxuriant vegetation. Not the gentle rolling hills I can see over the rooftops from my balcony, this is the real Cumbria, the wild, rocky mountains and deep, dangerous lakes. Deceptively cold even in midsummer, Wastwater is a magnet for hardy scuba divers with thick wetsuits rather than sailors, and the occasional angler. Mostly though, this is walking country, a place to come and simply absorb the bigness of the space, the emptiness, the silence. I adore it. This is why I live here, why I continue to live here.

The light is starting to fail, but we can still make out the sheep dotted around on the hillside across the lake, nimbly picking their way up and across the swell of the land in search of the best grazing. Nick pulls me closer, drapes his arm across my shoulders.

"Are you cold?"

His polite inquiry takes me by surprise, but I realize I have just shivered. I'm not cold though, definitely not. I shake my head, and he rubs his hand roughly up and down my bare arm.

"Good. Take your T-shirt off then, please."

I gape at him then back at the road. It might be late, but someone could drive along at any time. Or some hiker might be ambling this way en route back to his car, keen to wrap himself around a hot meal and not expecting to be treated to an eyeful of me. Nick waits, patiently, but his gaze is level and serious, and I know he means it.

"You're mine, Freya, for the time being. Remember? We have a deal. And you have gorgeous breasts, girl, so I want to look at them. And if it suits me to show them off to anyone else who happens to be around, I'll do that too. Understood?"

I close my eyes, take a couple of slow breaths. Yes, I do understand. And I know this is not just a test of obedience, or of my modesty, or a way of testing my boundaries. It's all of those things. And it's also a sharp reminder that I'm in training already, and anything can happen, at any time. And that my Dom is in charge, absolutely, whenever he chooses to exert his authority. I take one more breath then hook my fingers under the hem of my T-shirt. I draw it over my head.

He nods his approval as I stand before him, my breasts now only covered by my low cut, lacy bra. Not for long though.

"The bra too, please. Take it off, and then place it with your T-shirt by the car. Then come back here and present your breasts to me."

I do as I'm told, praying that no elderly couple out for a nice drive on this fine evening should come tootling around the bend in the road and catch sight of me strolling about the place topless. I'm no supermodel, but I could cause an accident. Well, maybe. I don't though, and I arrive back in front of Nick Hardisty unobserved by anyone but him and an indeterminate number of sheep. I assume the required position, remembering how he taught me it in room nine back at the Collared and Tied club.

He just observes for a few moments, and I stand still, utterly self-conscious, my ears attuned for even the most distant engine noise. There is none, and he continues to look at me, to admire me, I hope. At last, he reaches out, trails the backs of his fingers lazily along the underside of my left breast. He draws his hand upwards, lightly grazing my nipple, which puckers and swells, hardening instantly under his touch and the slightly cool, still air. He appears to note the transformation, studying my breasts intently before lifting his gaze to mine.

"Very pretty, Miss Stone. You can relax now. And, I think you *are* cold."

My hands now free, I make a see-saw gesture with my left hand to indicate maybe, and he smiles once more, slightly apologetic. But not so much so that he might allow me to put my clothes back on. "I'm sorry about that, but we'll be a few minutes yet."

We both glance up the road as the faint sound of an engine disturbs our solitude. My instinct is to turn around, turn my back to the intruders, or to step behind Nick, but he's having none of that. He lifts one finger to indicate I am not to move, and steps aside to allow an unrestricted view to whoever might be driving past.

It's an obedience test and a demonstration of his authority, his temporary ownership and right to display me if he chooses. And of the absolute requirement that I set aside my inhibitions at his command. I pass the test, never breaking eye contact with my Dom until the car, a little red Citroen, comes into view. In that moment Nick steps in front of me, close up, and pulls me in close to his chest, effectively hiding me from view until the Citroen cruises past and out of sight once more.

As soon as we're alone again, he releases me, smiling at my bewildered expression. "Excellent. You did well. You would have stayed in view as long as I instructed you to, no matter how embarrassed it made you feel. That's what I required, and it's enough for me to know that you intended to obey me."

At my continued frown of bemusement he goes on to explain further, "But it's all about consent, isn't it. You and I have both volunteered to be here, but who knows what the folks in that little red car would have wanted. Or chosen. Might have been a family with young children, or an elderly couple on their way to church. They haven't consented to anything, so we leave them out of it." Then, his mood switching instantly to one of playfulness, he grins broadly. "Now, let's see how you are at skimming stones. My best is seven bounces. What about you?"

I stare, shake my head in amazement as he turns away, stepping down to the water's edge and selecting a handful of small, flat stones. He holds his collection in his left fist as he looks back up at me, the glint of challenge sparkling in his gray eyes now. "Come on, Miss Stone. Select your weapons. If you can manage four bounces I might even agree to fuck you again this evening. Across the bonnet of your beautiful car. Would you like that, my sexy little sub?"

I nod, but hesitantly. It's the car thing. What if I dent it? But I don't let that stop me entering into the spirit of this game as I step forward then crouch beside him to choose some stones for myself. Incredibly, as long as it's only Nick Hardisty looking at me, I'm quite unconcerned about my state of semi-undress as I scour the shoreline for suitable stones and collect up a few likely candidates. I know exactly what I'm looking for, nice flat ones about the size of a fifty pence piece and upwards. I've done a lot of stone skimming over the years. Four bounces—piece of piss!

Well it would be, if not for Nick Hardisty's interference. Happy with my first crop of missiles I square up to the lake, standing a few feet from Nick, my back to him as I curl my middle finger carefully and precisely around the edge of my first stone, ready to hurl it skimming across the surface of the water. I don't hear his approach, and double up in self-defensive surprise as his hand snakes around me to catch my undefended nipple between his finger and thumb, just as I make my shot. He squeezes swiftly, the pain sharp and hard and over in a moment. The stone goes wide, clattering across the pebbled shoreline as I twist in his arms. He shrugs, releasing me, backing off, his hands spread wide in mocking apology.

"Sorry, beautiful. Force of habit. I'll try to keep my hands to myself. Please, continue..."

I do, and of course, he doesn't. The next ten minutes are spent with Nick laughing, groping me unashamedly, cheering and groaning at my stone-skimming efforts and their varied results. And I'm clapping and preening in smug delight as, despite his determined attempts at sabotage, I manage to score an astounding five bounces. Nick puts up a brave attempt, concentrating hard on the task as he realizes he's not up against a mere novice, but the best he can manage is six. Eventually we decide to settle for what we've achieved and make our way back to my car. His right arm is draped over my shoulders, and he uses his fingertips to lightly stroke and flick my right nipple as we stroll across the springy grass. I eye my pristine, maroon red bonnet nervously as we draw near. Surely he wouldn't? In more or less broad daylight?

He would. And it's not really daylight by now anyway. Mercifully he had the foresight to park the car with its nose pointing away from the road. And the lay-by is cut into the contours of the surrounding hills so we're unlikely to attract the attention of any more passing motorists. Still, his curt, "Drop your jeans and bend over the bonnet" causes me to gulp. But I do it. Of course I do it.

I kick off my pumps first. My jeans and briefs are soon beside them on the grassy banking in front of the car. Naked now, I lean forward to brace my hands on the low bonnet of the Vantage, my bottom conveniently raised for his perusal. He moves to stand behind me. "Spread your legs, Miss Stone. Open wide."

I do as I'm instructed.

"Wider, please." It seems I am not yet positioned to his satisfaction. He gently nudges my right foot with his to indicate I should widen my stance still further, then with no preamble, plunges three fingers deep into my pussy.

I flinch, but in surprise not pain. I'd expected, anticipated, more in the way of preparation. Even so, his slick, easy entry is evidence enough of my readiness for this. His other hand is resting lightly on my naked bum as he withdraws his fingers, then thrusts them sharply into me again. A couple of more quick thrusts then he slides them out, only to immediately replace his fingers with his cock. I arch my back in delight at the full, stretching feeling, the sensuality of containing him, being filled by him. I clench around his length, all concern for my paintwork now abandoned as I give myself over to the waves of lust now coursing wildly through my body. He sets a brisk, demanding rhythm, and my first orgasm ripples easily and quickly through me, delighting but not quite satisfying me. Not yet. I want more, need more.

And there is more. Slowing, he leans over me, reaching around and under me to caress my clit, his fingers gliding easily and smoothly past my inner lips to roll the sensitive bud between his thumb and forefinger. I gasp, my breath catching in my throat as the tumult of sensation starts up again, this time concentrating and coalescing under his fingers as he increases the pressure. He withdraws his cock until only the head remains inside my entrance, then he thrusts once more, deep and hard. I clench in response, seizing and gripping him as my own pleasure builds, heightened by his deep penetration as I soar once more toward release.

He straightens, his wonderful, skilled fingers leaving my clit, and I feel cheated, abandoned. I swivel my hips, clench my inner muscles in protest, and he immediately slaps my bottom. Hard enough to hurt. And to excite. I drop my head, utterly accepting, greedy for more, hopeful, for anything and everything. He knows it, he's picked his moment.

"I'm going to explore your sweet little virgin arse now. Okay, girl?"

I don't think, don't hesitate. I'm totally his. I just nod, not even sure he can see me. I guess he can, because he gently parts my buttocks with his palms, opening my anus for his examination. He continues to fuck me, his long strokes now slow, steady, solid and reassuring as I feel his gaze on my most intimate opening, my only remaining secret place.

"Just one finger, and I won't hurt you. I promise." His tone is soft, but with that thread of steel in it which I'm sure all Doms cultivate, but Nick Hardisty has polished to a fine art.

I believe him though, if he was going to hurt me he would have said that. So I relax, ready to let him do what he wants with me. To me.

It feels strange at first, the slight pressure as he inserts just the tip of one thoroughly slick and well-lubricated finger into my anus, my own juices serving their purpose as he gently but firmly pushes past the sphincter. My instinct is to resist, but I consciously fight that urge, responding to his deep but gentle penetration and the firm caress of his other palm on my buttock, smoothing away the slight sting of his slap a few moments ago.

The whole experience is intensely erotic, arousing, incredibly personal and intimate, and I feel tears threatening. Emotional, joyful tears — my connection to him, my absolute faith in him so overwhelming in that moment. He increases the pressure, working his finger farther into me, and I accept him, welcome him. I know when he's reached his full extent. His finger is now fully inserted and he starts to withdraw, only to ease slowly and surely back in again. He repeats the careful, deliberate movement, once more, twice, increasing his speed only slightly. Just enough to pick up the same rhythm as that set by his cock, fucking my pussy leisurely, at the same time finger-fucking my now totally receptive arse.

The unfamiliar sensations excite and intrigue, and the familiar warms and calms. It's enough, more than enough. Shivering and shuddering toward my climax, I'm intensely aware of his presence in me, everywhere, and of nothing else. In that moment I think a whole army of hikers could have ambled past and I'd not have known they were there.

Nick eases me tenderly and surely over the cliff and I'm tumbling, weightless and spinning as my release finally washes through me. It's fabulous, otherworldly, and I'm struck by how different it seems to be each time he does this to me, sometimes so powerful it takes my breath away, other times, like this, so achingly sweet I want to cry. Before, he made me sizzle, now I'm melting, soft and pliable and yielding. And totally fulfilled.

His finger leaves me as I regain my senses, and he snakes his other arm around my waist to hold me upright as my knees buckle. With a couple of swift, hard strokes, he finds his own climax. There's a muffled "Holy fuck, Freya" as his semen spurts out to fill the condom he somehow managed to bring into the mix without me even being aware of it.

We're breathing heavily as he at last straightens, withdrawing from me and quickly doing the necessary with the condom before reaching for me once more. He lifts and turns me, still helping me to stay upright as he lowers his head, intending to kiss me. Instead though, he sees the tears I was only dimly aware of, now flowing freely across my face. He stops, framing my face with his hands as he uses his thumbs to smooth them away.

"Tears, Freya? I didn't hurt you, did I?"

I shake my head, smiling ruefully as I wonder how I could possibly mime 'tears of joy'. I don't need to though, as he continues to hold my gaze, his slate eyes warm now, and tender. "I see."

He continues to wipe away my tears, and I couldn't stem the flow even if I'd tried to. He doesn't seem to mind, just waits until I'm collected, calmer. His kiss is brief, approving, before he straightens, catching and holding my gaze.

"This thing we're doing together is very intense, particularly for the sub who's just learning, exploring, finding out things about herself. It peels back your emotional layers, releases feelings you weren't even aware of. Crying's natural, and it's honest. If you feel you want to cry, then just do it. Don't try to fight it or hide it from me. And don't be embarrassed. This is just me, and I know what's going on. It helps me to know how it's affecting you, how I'm making you feel. Especially when you can't easily tell me any other way. Okay?"

His voice is quiet, muted in this vast space around us as his words are only intended to reach my ears, no further. His face, beautifully masculine, the Dominant severity now veiled under genuine concern and tenderness, is just inches from mine. I can see the lighter flecks in his storm gray eyes as he continues to hold my gaze, connecting with me, this moment every bit as intimate as when his fingers and cock were buried deep inside me.

I nod, my tremulous smile still somewhat watery as he lowers his head to kiss me properly at last. It's a long, dragging kiss, deep and sensual and totally absorbing. I cling to him as I try to convey my absolute and bone-deep gratitude for the things he's showing me, teaching me.

He breaks the kiss at last, raising his head to catch my gaze.

"Tears aside, I'm guessing you liked that. All of it."

It's a statement, not a question, but I nod my agreement anyway.

He dips his head in acknowledgment. "And you learned from it. I think your boundaries have shifted a lot today. You are a very receptive student, Miss Stone. And so am I. Would you demonstrate the signing for 'thank you', please?" He steps back slightly to allow me room to move my hands.

Puzzled, I nevertheless demonstrate the gesture, touching my fingers to my lips before extending my open hand.

He nods, and repeats it back to me. Thanking me for the lesson?

"When I teach you something, you should thank me. So from now on, I expect to see that gesture a lot, Miss Stone. And when I correct your behavior too, when I punish you and you learn from it. You will thank me for that as well. Now, teach me 'please', if you would be so kind." His tone has hardened now, cooled, the Dom voice is back, and once more his mercurial switches unnerve me.

I demonstrate the correct sign. He inclines his head, storing the information. "I expect you to be respectful at all times, assume the proper attitude from a submissive toward her Dom. So you will ask me nicely when you want something, I expect to be seeing a lot of 'please' and 'thank you'. I demand perfect manners from my submissive. And you will need to say sorry when you make a mistake, so now show me how you'll say 'I apologize'."

This time I touch my mouth before making a fist and rubbing it on my other palm, instinctively assuming the downcast eyes and anxious facial expression that would usually accompany the gesture. He notices the whole combination, and takes my chin between his palms to lift my face, bringing my eyes back to meet his once more.

"Eye contact will be an issue for us. Usually I'd require a submissive to lower her eyes, especially when showing respect, or when she's being disciplined. But your eyes are so expressive. They tell me how you're feeling, and I need those signals from you. We'll see how that goes, but generally I want you to look at me, not the floor. Is that clear?"

I nod, and he tilts his head wryly.

"One more key word for now. You'll call me 'Sir'. At all times, please. So show me how that should look."

I think for a moment, the nearest approximation dragged up from my school days although this seems not exactly the same sense of the word. Still, it'll have to do. I demonstrate the gesture, then, on impulse, I also sign 'master'. He watches, then regards me carefully. "Are those words interchangeable?" Insightful and intuitive as ever, he knows just what to ask me.

I shrug, wrinkle my nose to indicate 'not really'.

He nods curtly. "Then I think the first will be fine." In a rapid shift of mood, he leans down to pick up my discarded jeans and briefs, handing them to me. "Now, I've worked up an appetite. For food. What about you?"

I nod. In fact I'm famished. Apart from a few cups of coffee, I've not eaten all day. I balance on one leg as I wriggle back into my jeans, and Nick Hardisty, 'Sir' to me now, it seems, strolls around to the back of the car to collect my bra and T-shirt from where I placed them earlier. Coming back, he hands those to me as well.

"There's a nice pub at the far end of the lake. Have you been there?"

I have, many times, and I nod my approval of his choice. The Wasdale Head Inn is a wonderful moorland pub, a mecca for hikers and campers, and does a roaring trade in thick hot soup and chunky sandwiches. They know just the sort of fuel required to sustain the most intrepid fell walker across miles of the most brutal terrain in the country. I daresay they'll be able to come up with something to see me through my own challenges.

By the time my T-shirt is back in place and I'm thoroughly decent once more, Nick — sorry, 'Sir' — has the passenger door open and is waiting for me to slide back into the car. I do, belting myself in as my thoughts turn to chunky wholemeal bread and the rather acceptable bowl of carrot and parsnip broth I once guzzled on a previous visit.

'Sir' settles into the driver's seat once more and hits the button for launch control. He slants a mischievous glance in my direction. "There's nowhere else they could have been going, this road's a dead end. And they haven't come back this way yet. So, I wonder if your fan club in the red Citroen will recognize you with your clothes on..."

I gape at him, my eyes widening. I shake my head briefly, they couldn't have, didn't. Did they? He just laughs, reversing the Vantage smoothly back out onto the tarmac as two impassive sheep watch our progress from the brow of a nearby rise, clearly contemplating the vagaries of humans and perhaps relieved that we're leaving them in peace once more.

Understanding my consternation perfectly, 'Sir' continues, "There was a little wobble as they went around the bend, maybe. Perhaps just a glimpse, not enough to be sure..."

Chapter Nine

My fan club *is* waiting for us at the Wasdale Head, a middle-aged couple with their elderly mother it looks like, comfortably ensconced in a corner of the bar tucking into slabs of home-made meat and potato pie. We recognized their car in the car park as Nick slid the Vanquish into the adjacent space, and they are the only other occupants of the public room. The evening trade won't really build up for another hour or so, and the day trippers are all gone.

We nod politely to the red Citroen brigade as we pass their table and settle for a secluded booth by the window. Nick goes to the bar to order coffees and food. I select a tasty Beouf Bourgignon with rice, whilst he follows the example set by the occupants of the red Citroen and goes for a slab of meat and potato pie. By the time our meal arrives, all fragrant and steaming, I'm absolutely famished and dive into mine with a level of enthusiasm little short of gluttonous. Nick finds the whole thing hilarious, observing that it's encouraging to see I have a good, healthy appetite, that he hasn't managed to put me off my food. Yet.

Hardly likely.

The rest of the evening is spent chatting over nothing much at all. We have more coffee then I have a couple of glasses of dry white wine. Nick sticks to iced water, as he's insisting on driving back. I just shrug, let him have his way. I suspect I always will.

I take advantage of the moment to ask him something that's been puzzling me since our meeting in Costa.

Why did you agree to train me after all? What made you change your mind?

He regards me seriously for a few moments, and I get the impression he's not altogether sure of the answer to that. Eventually though he does volunteer an explanation.

"I like you. And I saw potential in you that night at the club. Despite my initial impression, you *are* a natural submissive. With proper training you could be superb."

I nod, thinking that's all I'm going to get, but it seems he hasn't entirely finished.

"I think you overstate your, what? Your vulnerability?" He glances at me quizzically.

I shrug. That's a good enough way of describing my situation I suppose. He continues. "You do have difficulties, I accept that, and some things need to be done differently with you. For you. But not that much, not really. You just need time, and patience, and I know now how rewarding you can be. Your orgasms are so sweet, all that gasping and panting and clenching around my cock."

He smiles at me, his eyes warm, sexy, and my toes curl. Still he hasn't finished. "All Doms should be patient, and take particular care of an inexperienced sub, but unfortunately not all are. And you, you're just an accident waiting to happen. I was worried about you, about what you might try next. And who with. But make no mistake, Freya, I wanted to train you. If I didn't, I would never have agreed. I'm here because I want to be, just as you are."

Wow. Nice answer. Mostly. And so not what I expected. I reach for my phone again.

Doesn't it spoil it, for you? Me making no sounds? I thought Doms liked that sort of feedback. That they liked to hear a sub scream.

He smiles, shakes his head. "As I've said, it's different with you. And more complex than that. Your responses are exquisite, Freya, it makes my mouth water just thinking about how delightful you are when you come. And you shouldn't ever let anyone suggest otherwise. If you do ever hear a putdown like that from a Dom, you're in the hands of an idiot, which is never good, and you need to be out of there. Yes?"

I gaze at him, and nod. He's so good for my self-esteem.

By the time we've finished our drinks the bar is filling up nicely. For such a secluded spot, this pub seems to do a roaring trade. There's no chance of seclusion now so I'm not surprised really when Nick asks me if I'm ready to leave. By mutual consent we prefer our privacy. We stroll back across the now busy car park hand in hand and I'm oddly pleased when Nick opens my car door for me and hands me in.

Old fashioned courtesy as well as spanking—what a delightful combination.

By nine o'clock we're gliding to a halt, back in my personal parking bay once more. Nick walks with me as far as the lift then stops. Turning me to face him he drops another light kiss onto my lips. "I'll leave you here, if that's all right. I have things to do, things to be sorting out for my trip. I'll be away for at least a month, but I *will* be in touch. Watch out for my texts and respond immediately. No excuses, okay? And I'll set up your appointments for you."

I'm disappointed, I had wondered if he might decide to come back in, maybe even stay over, but I always knew that was unlikely. So I nod, accepting, and as an afterthought sign, "Thank you, Sir."

He inclines his head, one Dom-like eyebrow raised in approval. "Excellent manners, Miss Stone. You are an impressive student. I'm looking forward to when we next meet."

And with that, he's gone, strolling casually over to his huge motor bike, which I now spot tucked away in a visitor's space at the other side of the parking area. I must ask him when he parked it there, though I assume it had to be before he met me at the Costa coffee shop. He must have been confident he'd end up here.

Doms are so cocky.

* * * *

I receive a brief text from Nick the following morning telling me to present myself at the *Pretty Things* salon for waxing at four o'clock this same afternoon, and that I have an appointment with the club medic the following morning. I text back immediately to thank him, remember to call him 'Sir' and confirm I'll be there. Then I get on the Qantas website to book my flight to Australia for the day after that.

I research Brazilian waxing on the Internet before I go along to the salon, and even find a very explicit video so I know exactly what to expect. The video advises two max strength Anadin's half an hour before, and a long soak in the bath. I prepare accordingly, but despite my precautions I'm still cringing as I present myself at the glass reception desk in the entrance to the salon. The receptionist is pleasant and welcoming, inviting me to take a seat for a moment and assuring me I won't have a long wait. She picks up the phone on the desk and speaks into it.

"Mike, your ten o'clock's here."

Mike! Surely not...

My desperate hope that Mike might actually turn out to be Michelle, or even Michaela are dashed when my attendant pops out of a room to my right. At just under six feet, sporting a neatly trimmed mustache, and biceps that bear witness to many hours spent in the gym, Mike is most definitely not short for Michaela.

"Miss Stone? This way please..." His tone is efficient and friendly.

But there's no way I can see myself spreading my legs and letting him wax my pubic hair. *Christ!*

I just gape at him, wondering how to explain. How to request a female beautician. Seeing my flustered expression he stops, waiting at the door to his domain.

"Is there a problem, Miss Stone?" This from the friendly receptionist, still perched at her station and watching the proceedings.

I glance back at her, surely she'll understand. Apparently not. "Mike's one of our best beauticians.

And Mr Hardisty did specify that your attendant should be a male..."

Ah. It all becomes clear. Well, clearer. This is another test of my submission, a demonstration of his authority. He knew I'd hate this. The procedure is bad enough as it is, painful enough, without the added humiliation of having to strip, open my legs and let a man touch me so intimately. And that's exactly why he set it up this way. I close my eyes, draw a deep breath and follow Mike into his little cubicle.

"Mr Hardisty specified an all over wax so I'll need you to strip completely please."

Mike's polite, efficient and completely professional. I can do no less than return the compliment. A few moments later I stand naked before his dispassionate gaze as he examines me for all and every wisp of unwanted body hair. My underarms, legs, all are to be carefully and completely smoothed, utterly hair-free. He snaps on his latex gloves and lays me on his treatment table. He turns me one way, then the other, applying his wax and fabric strips and ripping away the offending hairs mercilessly.

When it comes to my pubic hair he asks me to bend one knee, bringing my heel right up to my bum, then he gently presses my knee to the side, opening me for his work. He offers me one brief smile of reassurance before bending and concentrating on his task, deftly smoothing on the wax then sharply ripping it away to tear out the hairs.

He's quick, I have to grant him that. And clearly his reputation as one of the salon's best beauticians is well deserved. I lie there while he works, concentrating on breathing deeply, not wriggling, and offering no protest no matter how intimately he touches me. It's particularly difficult when he politely asks me to crouch on all fours, my knees spread wide as he gently parts my buttocks to spread the wax around my anus. I'm not sure if the salon staff will be reporting back to Nick, but I wouldn't be surprised and I'm determined not to disgrace myself. I comply with every request without fuss. If Nick Hardisty wants me to do this, to endure this humiliation, I will. For him.

At last my treatment is complete. Mike smoothes baby oil all over my smarting, tender skin and offers me a mirror to inspect my newly smooth nether regions. Past embarrassment now, I thank him and take a close look. He's done a good job, I can see that. I have to admit I really do look rather nice down there — all pretty and pink and very obvious. My clit is now on proud display, and I can only shiver at the thought of how much more prominent it will become when I'm aroused. I've already noticed that several subs at the club remove their pubic hair and that Doms seem to like it — now I can see why.

* * * *

I drive to Lancaster to see the doctor at her private surgery. She's already accessed my medical records so is familiar with my aphonia. I'm offered a signing interpreter when I present myself at the reception desk, but I decline. I'd really prefer not to have a third person present, and can generally manage by writing stuff down. I wonder whether Nick had mentioned the possible need for an interpreter, another example of his thinking ahead and anticipating what I might need, or maybe the doctor just worked it out from my medical history. I resolve to ask him.

The doctor is also aware of my diabetes, and agrees with me that it's under control and not likely to cause me any problems in my coming encounter with Nick Hardisty. Picking up on my communication issues, it's clear that she understands the precise nature of our planned activities and the potential risks. She stresses, as Nick had, the importance of body language and using other signals to let my Dom know how I'm feeling. But like him, she doesn't seem unduly worried about that aspect of things.

She asks me questions about my menstrual cycle, does a pregnancy test just to make sure, takes a number of blood samples, weighs and measures me, then does an internal examination before pronouncing me fit for purpose. She promises to send the results to Nick, as agreed, and to forward to me the results of his blood tests in due course.

I come out of her surgery feeling great, oddly elated, and head home to finish my packing.

* * * *

All the way to Australia, as I count the minutes ticking by on the long, long flight to Singapore. All through the seemingly never-ending second leg of the journey into Kingsford Smith airport, my head is teeming with the details of my recent encounters with Nick Hardisty. And even more compelling, the encounters to come, after my return to the UK. I turn over in my mind how much of my kinky lifestyle I could possibly share with Margaret, and to what end? Sharing might be good, but I'm not in need of advice, my mind is made up. I'm committed, and not for a moment regretting the decision I've made. I've wanted this, so badly wanted this. And now, I'm to have my wish.

I'm not convinced Margaret would understand my unusual sexual preferences. Summer certainly doesn't and I've had years to try to explain. Or maybe Margaret would—she seems to understand everything, and she always 'got' me, right from the beginning. But still…

Seeing my adored foster-mother again is wonderful, and as ever I'm delighted that she seems so happy. No one deserves happiness more than she does, and not for the first time I bless the day I won that money and found myself in a position to help her make the leap to grab this new life of hers. I ponder over whether to tell her what my plans are for when I return home, but eventually decide against it. She's never likely to meet Nick, and I somehow don't think she shares my fascination with kinky sexual adventures. So we settle for five weeks of good food, swimming, shopping, theater and the rest of what New South Wales has to offer.

Sydney is a beautiful city, one of the loveliest I have ever seen, although admittedly my travel experience is not yet especially wide. I'm getting there though, but I have yet to develop a real fondness for traveling alone. Apart from the world-famous harbor area dominated by the magnificent and iconic opera house, the city has wonderful beaches and watersports to rival anything in the world.

I'll never tire of watching humpback whales and dolphins, and although I'm not a strong swimmer, I love this beach-based lifestyle. But the shops are my real passion, and Margaret and I spend countless hours that trip in the boutiques and arcades as I replenish my not inconsiderable wardrobe. I recall

Nick's suggestion that I make sure to pack plenty of seductive underwear for my stay at his home, and if Margaret wonders why the pile of skimpy lace and satin objects in my guest room at her house just keeps on growing, she's too polite to comment. Or maybe she does have an inkling—I'm twenty-three years old after all, it's about time I started putting it about a bit.

We book one of our regular trips to the Outback, a few days of intense heat, arid dust, rocks and an infinity of scorching emptiness at the Mungo National Park. This must be one of the most beautiful and the most cruelly demanding places on the planet, but I love it. I never tire of gazing across the desert landscape and recalling my earliest memories of the endless sands of Morecambe Bay. I now know the difference between that and a true desert, but the memories it evokes are powerful and we spend much of my trip reminiscing about the UK. Margaret loves her new partner and her new life, but never tires of talking about 'home'.

The weeks slip by rapidly, a blur of sightseeing and retail therapy. Most powerful of all though is the sheer joy of being reunited with Margaret. We chat, we reminisce. She asks after Summer, enquires about what quilting projects I have on the go, shows me what she's working on. I rummage through her box of UFOs—unfinished objects—and we spend the evenings companionably as I put the final touches to some of her projects. Despite my generally chaotic approach to housekeeping, I do have a thing about finishing what I start. It's just like old times, but warmer. Not so wet.

Then it's over. Before I know it, the five weeks have passed. Margaret and George are helping me to pile my luggage into the back of their car and driving me back to the airport. I cling to Margaret at the entrance to the departure lounge, the huge plate glass doors swishing backwards and forwards behind me as other passengers hurry through, rushing along at the start of their journeys. I know it won't be that long before I see Margaret again, but even so this does feel like a pivotal moment. As though something fundamental is changing. Perhaps it is.

I tear myself away and sling my hand luggage over my shoulder. I walk through the doors, then turn to wave at the two women. George has draped an arm around Margaret's shoulders and I can see that Margaret is crying. So am I. I wipe the tears from my own face and manage a tremulous smile before I start to make my way toward the banks of soft seating. I'm quickly swallowed by the crowds, and when I look back again the sea of people hides Margaret from view. I'm on my way home.

* * * *

And now, I *am* home. After a five week stay in New South Wales, and after being on the move for twenty-four hours, I'm at last stepping off the Qantas jet at Manchester. I breathe in the familiar chilly air and glance up at the gray skies before moving along into the airbridge. Spots of rain are pattering against the roof of the tunnel as I troop through with the other first class passengers, heading for the main terminal building. Passport control and baggage reclaim are necessary evils of international travel and I do what I need to do before finally emerging with my suitcase into the damp early evening an hour or so later. I wait my turn for a taxi, and eventually I'm settled in the back seat heading for home. And Nick Hardisty.

I didn't hear from him at all for the first three weeks. Then I received a text reminding me of the date our month together is to start. I acknowledged it and confirmed I'd be there. A couple of days later I received another text, this time advising me of Nick's address and providing directions to find his home. I was surprised to find that he lives near me, in Cartmel, only about ten miles from Kendal. I acknowledged that message too.

The next text informed me that my wax treatment from nearly six weeks ago would need to be repeated, and that he'd made arrangements with Mike to attend to me the day after my return to the UK. I confirmed my intention to keep the appointment, kicking myself for not appreciating that the effects would be relatively short-lived and would need to be replenished. I might as well not have bothered with the first ordeal. Of course, Nick knew full well that this would happen, hence the pre-booked appointment.

The next message asked me to arrive at Nick's home at three o'clock in the afternoon on the appointed date, and to bring only a small bag with essential toiletries and any medical requirements. And he reminded me that my clothing requirements will be minimal.

A potential problem has arisen though, or more accurately the problem had only just occurred to me. I was somewhat nervous as I replied to that latest text.

My apologies, Sir. I've just realized I'll be having my period when I arrive and it will continue for three days into my training. Would you prefer to delay?

His response is typically blunt.

No delay. This was likely to be an issue at some point. Will you be in any discomfort?

No, Sir, not usually.

Good. It makes no difference then. By the end of our time together this issue will probably arise again, and by that time I will require a more relaxed attitude from you.

Thank you for your understanding. I expect I'll be perfectly well, Sir. And relaxed. I'm happy to proceed as planned.

His reply was typically succinct.

Excellent. Don't be late.

And now, as I sit in the back of the taxi, purring up the M6 toward Cumbria once more, I know it's only two more days and one excruciating wax treatment before I see him again.

And it all starts.

Chapter Ten

Two fifty-seven. I pull up outside Nick Parrish's house about half a mile out of Cartmel and heave a sigh of relief. I'm on time. I took the precaution of checking out the address on Google maps and set off early, but still I've been dreading his reaction if I should be even a few seconds late. This is a big deal, much bigger than the coffee shop in Kendal. I get out of my car and gaze in some surprise at the property. It's not what I expected.

To start with, the place is huge. It's a long, sprawling, slate built bungalow surrounded by a five foot wall. Impressive wrought iron gates open onto a cobbled courtyard where my lovely Vanquish is now lording it in glorious isolation. I'd expected to see Nick's motor cycle here, or maybe a car. I guess he must have a car. But there's no other vehicle except mine. The place looks deserted. I double check my map and the address. I'm supposed to be at a place called Edge End Farm, and I glance back at the gate post to check. Yes, the name plate there confirms I seem to have arrived at the right place. So, where is he?

I walk up to the front door, a pretty shade of red, and knock. I wait. No answer. I knock again, louder. Still no response. I go back to my car and reach in to find my bag. I drag my phone out to double check the required date and time—you never know...

I see that there's another message, just arrived. It's from Nick.

I'm delayed. Key at Post office in village. Make yourself at home. Please stay there until I arrive.

To think I managed to get all the way back from Australia in time to keep our appointment, then busted a gut to make sure I was on time today. Seems like it's another rule for Doms, as ever. Still, there's no alternative. With a sigh I hop back in my car and head down into Cartmel. I find the post office easily enough and soon retrieve the key to Edge End Farm from the motherly type behind the counter. She eyes me curiously, especially when I hand her a note across the counter like some sort of clichéd bank robber, but obviously she concludes I look harmless enough, and I daresay she has her instructions to hand over the keys so she does just that. I pocket them, nod my thanks, smile my agreement to pass on her regards to Nick then make my way back to Nick's house to let myself in.

At first sight Nick Parrish's house really is as nice inside as it is on the outside. I haul my modest bag in from the boot of my car, mostly crammed with seductive underwear and toiletries, and drop it on the floor inside the front door before setting off on my solitary tour.

His text said to make myself at home, so the first thing I should do is to find my way around. The rooms seem to go off a central hallway, thickly carpeted, and I stroll down it, curious and opening doors. I'm delighted to find a large, very well equipped kitchen, and look forward to maybe getting to do some of the cooking in it. Apart from quilting, I have a passion for food and cooking, possibly the result of my diabetes. My dietary needs mean it's easier to cook healthy food for myself from scratch rather than rely on processed food or eating out.

As soon as I was diagnosed, aged fifteen, Margaret made it her business to instil in me an appreciation for fresh fruit, vegetables and all things diabetic friendly. A brief glance in Nick Parrish's fridge and cupboards is heartening, he's stocked the place with suitable food, lots of things I can eat. I don't know whether this is his normal preference or whether he's taken the trouble to find out what my needs are and has bought these items especially for me. I find myself hoping it's the latter.

I continue my exploration, finding a dining room, a comfortable lounge with a huge wall-mounted television, a utility room, three bedrooms, one with en suite facilities, and a house bathroom. There's a large conservatory at the rear and a door leading to a large, new-looking extension. That door's locked, but having exhausted all other possibilities, I'm reasonably certain that behind this door is Nick Parrish's dungeon. He must have one—he wouldn't have insisted we spend the month here otherwise.

I wander back along the corridor and find myself in the kitchen. I decide to help myself to a cup of tea, and start rummaging in cupboards to find the necessary bits and pieces. I dig out a mug to use and find some teabags in a cupboard. I press the switch on the electric kettle and wait, listening to the friendly hiss and fizzle as it heats. My phone pings again, another text.

Sorry. I'll be a while yet. Please make yourself comfortable, help yourself to anything you want.

I press reply.

Should I come back a bit later? It's all right. Really.

The response is immediate. Unambiguous.

No. Stay there.

I sip my tea as I wander back through the house, finally ending up in the lounge. I find the remote control and turn on the huge television, idly flicking through channels and finding nothing to interest me. How much longer? He's given no indication of how long he expects to be delayed for. Should I be expecting him in the next hour or so? This evening? Tonight? Tomorrow? I pull out my phone to text him back.

Any idea when you'll be here?

His response is curt.

No

Right. I make myself another cup of tea and try to interest myself in late afternoon quiz shows as I watch the clock hands creeping around. I kick off my shoes and tuck my feet under me as I snuggle up on the huge sofa in the lounge. I watch the news, the early evening soaps, and still he doesn't come. I don't dare text him again. Do I? But now he's five hours late. Maybe something's gone wrong. Is he okay?

At nine o'clock I text him again.

Is everything OK?

The response comes at ten past ten.

Yes. I'll see you when I get there.

When do you think that might be? Should I come back tomorrow?

What part of Stay There is not clear to you?

Oddly hurt, I reply.

Sorry. Of course. I'll see you soon.

Nick did not specify which bedroom I should use, and I'm not sure what he'll expect, except that he did mention we'd be sleeping together when he laid out the terms of our 'deal'. It's clear from the clutter of belongings on the dressing table and male toiletries in the en suite which of the three bedrooms is his, and eventually I decide to take a chance and use that one. I can't imagine he'll throw me out of his bed if he turns up during the night. At eleven thirty I slide, alone, between his sheets and try to sleep.

At three o'clock, still alone, I get up and head back to the kitchen to make myself yet another cup of tea. I fall asleep, at last, at the kitchen table, at five o'clock in the morning.

* * * *

It's after nine when I wake up, stiff and cold, and still alone. I wander back to Nick's room to shower in his en suite facilities and get dressed. No word from him overnight, and I'm really nervous about contacting him after his last curt message. I'm sure this is some sort of test, but what am I supposed to be doing? Or maybe he's genuinely been held up on his business trip. Maybe things haven't gone smoothly. Maybe, maybe, maybe.

By eleven I'm climbing the walls, there's only so much you can do to pass the time alone in a strange house. Especially when you don't care for television and didn't even bring a book. I wish I'd brought my sewing machine. I did think of asking if I could, but thought probably not. We'd be too busy. I hoped. I never expected to spend nearly twenty-four hours alone.

By twelve I'm bored almost literally to tears, confused and lonely. I want my own home, my own stuff. And at last, in a pit of lonely, miserable boredom, I eventually decide to do it. To do what's been hovering at the edge of my mind for hours now. I'm going to nip home to collect my sewing machine and latest quilting project. Then I can keep myself occupied until he comes. Kendal's only a couple of miles away, well, ten. I can be back within the hour. I wish I'd thought of this last night.

Purposeful at last, I grab my car keys from the kitchen worktop and head outside. I lock Nick's front door carefully behind me and get into my car. As I pull out of his gate I remember his clear instruction that I stay at his house and wait for him, but surely he didn't mean me to sit tight for so long. He can't have known he'd be delayed all night when he told me to stay put. Sooner or later I'd have to do something else. He must realize that. And twenty-four hours is a long time to wait for someone...

I'm back within the hour, my sewing machine and quilting paraphernalia safely stowed in the boot of my car. I'm relieved — and disappointed — to find there's still no motor cycle or car in the cobbled courtyard as I pull up. I let myself back inside, not bothering even to unload my gear from the boot. With a sigh I flick the switch on the kettle once more and start to fix myself yet another cup of tea.

At three o'clock in the afternoon I still haven't brought my sewing machine inside, and I'm not entirely sure why I thought I needed it. Seated once more at the kitchen table, I nibble my way through a chicken salad. I glance back at the clock on the cooker, for what must be about the thousandth time today, just as I hear a faint click in the hallway.

The door. He's here. At last!

I rush out of the kitchen into the hallway, to see Nicholas Hardisty depositing his crash helmet on a side table. He glances at me, smiles briefly before shrugging out of his leather biker jacket and hanging that up on one of a row of hooks beside his door. His casual black T-shirt and faded blue Levi's look incongruously ordinary and at the same time both sexy and menacing on him as he fixes his gray gaze on me. He waits a few moments before speaking, as though considering what, how much, to say to me.

"Sorry to be late. Something came up. Are you all right? Did you find everything you need?"

I nod. Then shake my head. I'm confused, and upset. Is this all he has to say? I shrug and frown, opening my hands in a gesture of query. Surely he owes me some sort of explanation.

Apparently he thinks not.

"Excuse me?" His imperious glance lets me know in no uncertain terms he has no intention of explaining himself to me.

Recklessly perhaps, in this moment I don't think that's anywhere near good enough. I head back into the kitchen for my phone. He may not want to talk to me, but I have plenty I want to say to him. He follows me in there as I'm fumbling with the phone, flicks the kettle on again and reaches for a mug.

"Tea?" He glances at me over his shoulder as he drops a teabag into his mug.

I ignore him, all tea'd out for now, and continue to tap my barrage of questions into the phone.

"If you want to talk to me, sign it."

What?

I stop typing, look at him in confusion.

He turns to face me, his hands moving, the gestures familiar. "If you have something to say, use sign." His hands are slow, unpracticed, but it's BSL. My language.

He's signing, he's learned my language. I couldn't be more astonished if he'd sprouted wings and started flapping around the room.

I gape at him as he repeats his statement, and at last I respond, my hands flying in easy, rapid-fire signing, "How? When did you learn that?"

He smiles. "You're too fast for me, I'm a novice. Slow down."

I do, repeating my questions slowly.

His response is stilted, slow, but clearly recognizable. "I've been busy too while you were in Australia. So, no excuses now. You can talk to me."

I can. I really can. I step forward, my temper evaporating. Which is probably for the best, not sensible to start an argument with an already grumpy Dom. I'm unsure how to express what this gesture means to me. Not only has he bought me food I can eat, but he's gone to all this trouble, just to help me, one of just a handful of people who have. On impulse I stand before him, lift my hand and stroke his cheek. I smile, and reach up to kiss him on the mouth. He dips his face toward mine, wraps one arm around my back, pulls me in close as he takes over, deepens the kiss.

I forget my annoyance at his cavalier treatment, his high-handedness regarding the waxing treatments, his insistence that I be punctual and available, only to show up himself whenever it suited him. All rational thought is driven from my mind as his tongue snakes into my mouth, probing and exploring and arousing. His palms are firm and hard, caressing my bottom, lifting me and bringing me closer for his exploration. In moments my skirt is raised, bunched around my waist as he firmly molds and shapes my responsive buttocks. He slides his fingers under my thong from behind, swiftly penetrating me as I loop my arms around his neck and hang on.

I'm slick and wet and clench around the two, possibly three fingers inside me as he curls them to find and hit my most sensitive spot. I'm shuddering, my arousal spiraling, rushing toward orgasm when he suddenly stops. He lifts his head, withdraws his teasing, tantalizing fingers from my greedy, disappointed body. He straightens, steps away to regard me sternly. Something's wrong, something has changed, but I don't know what, or how.

My expression no doubt eloquently communicating my confusion, and my frustration, I watch him warily. At last I can stand it no longer.

"What's the matter?" I sign, remembering to make the gestures slowly, deliberately.

This time he answers verbally. "Who are you talking to?"

I look at him, confused for a moment, then I remember. I sign the word for 'Sir', then for 'sorry'.

He nods briefly. "I don't want to have to keep reminding you. If you need me to make the lesson more memorable though, I will. So, did you obey my instructions, girl?"

I nod, slowly, trying to remember. My frown indicates my uncertainty, my confusion.

"Are you sure? Think carefully, girl." The Dom voice, sharp, hard, cold, his glacial eyes pinning me in place.

There's something, he's aware of something, some transgression or omission. My stomach clenches, but not with lust this time. Now it's apprehension, bone-deep and paralyzing, my confidence shredding under his withering stare. Not for the first time, I wonder how it is that Doms manage to do that, instil terror with just a look, just a glance.

And it's not so much that I'm afraid of his punishment if I *have* somehow managed to fall short of his requirements, not live up to his expectations. My despair stems from the awful, gnawing sense that I've somehow managed inadvertently to disappoint him. I so want to please him, to gain his approval. I've read about this. And now I'm experiencing it for real. I've read enough literature, fictional and otherwise, about this lifestyle I'm trying so hard to espouse and adopt, to know that a Dom/sub relationship is psychological as well as physical. Maybe more so. And whatever the agreement between us, whatever its purpose, its limits and its precise terms, emotionally I'm responding to him submissively, as my Dom. It's really that simple.

Cowed, I wait. And wait. He's giving nothing away, no clues or hints. Not yet. He simply regards me, patient, impassive. And relentless.

At last, "I asked you to stay here, to wait for me. Did you do as I asked?"

I drop my eyes, only to have him cup my chin in his palm and force my gaze back to his. "I told you, eye contact unless I say otherwise. Now, girl, did you do as I asked? Yes or no?"

I feel tears pricking behind my eyes. I see his gorgeous, stern, unforgiving face shimmer and blur as the tears distort my vision. It never once occurs to me to attempt to deceive him. He knows anyway, somehow he knows I went out. I was only gone for an hour or so, and there's no clue left indoors to suggest I made a return trip to my home. My sewing machine and other quilting bits and pieces are safely secreted in the boot of my car, never having even been unloaded. But even so, he knows.

My lips are trembling as I shake my head, indicating 'no', I didn't obey his instructions.

He drops his hand from my chin, steps back to lean on the worktop, reaching behind him for his mug of tea. He lifts it to his lips, watching me closely over the rim of the mug as he sips his drink.

"So, Freya, tell me in what way you disobeyed me. And why you did that." His tone chilling, forbidding. Utterly daunting.

Despite his instructions my gaze drops to the floor once more, only to be dragged sharply back. "Look at me. Look away again, and I *will* punish you for it, Freya. Now, tell me, in what way did you disobey my instructions?"

I hesitate, and he settles himself more comfortably against the worktop. Deceptively so.

"I'm running out of patience, girl. Get on with it."

"I didn't stay here. You told me to wait for you here, but I went out. I'm sorry, Sir." My agile, practiced hands sign the words, slowly and clearly.

He watches me carefully, his understanding apparent in his piercing eyes. "Where did you go? And why?"

"I went home, Sir. To collect some items, some things I forgot."

"What things?"

"My sewing machine, Sir, and my quilting things."

"Why did you need those?"

"I was bored, you weren't here and I thought…" My hands drop and I clench them loosely in front of me as his withering gaze releases me at last to rake around the room. Then he's back, pinning me with his eyes once more.

"So where is it then? This sewing machine that you needed so urgently, and the other stuff?"

I hesitate, knowing that leaving my belongings apparently hidden in my car boot will only serve to make it appear that I was trying to conceal them. And with chilling self-awareness I realize that this is exactly why they did remain in the car. I knew he'd be angry and I didn't want to have to face that. With a sinking sense of regret I now begin to realize that not only has he drawn out my confession to having disobeyed him, but with my next answer he'll know I also attempted to deceive him too.

There's no avoiding the issue though, so I sign my response. "They're in the boot of my car, Sir. I never brought them inside."

"Why not?"

I take my time, considering my response to that. My first instinct is to tell him I didn't have time, that he came back before I had the opportunity to bring my machine inside and set it up. But the problem is, that's not the truth. The truth is I knew he'd spot it, even if I managed to tidy up and put everything away, there'd be some clue left behind. Some stray length of thread or snippet of fabric, some pin or scrap of paper. So I left my quilting equipment safely hidden from him, in the boot of my car. And I honestly thought I'd get away with it. What an idiot.

I take a deep breath, look him in the eye and sign my response, "I didn't want you to know I had it here, Sir. I was hiding it. And I'm truly sorry."

His gaze never wavers as he continues to regard me coldly. Long seconds tick by, and every instinct within me demands that I drop my eyes, turn away, run. Anything to escape that intensely disappointed, dissatisfied expression now clouding his beautiful face. At last he places his mug, now empty, on the worktop alongside him and steps forward. He takes my face between his palms, ignoring the tears now coursing down my cheeks. He makes no attempt to stem them, to offer me any words of comfort, forgiveness, acceptance.

"I intend to punish you, Freya, because you have to learn obedience. That's a fundamental part of your training. As your trainer, I need to correct your behavior, and for this I have no option but to discipline you. However your last answer spared you the severe punishment I was planning for you if you'd continued your attempts at deception. I do appreciate that you told me the truth. Eventually. Do you understand that, Freya? And do you understand why I have to punish you now?"

I nod.

"Good. And do you accept your punishment?"

I nod again, as his eyes narrow thoughtfully. "And what punishment do you consider would be fitting on this occasion, Freya?" He lowers his hands, releasing my face. I step slightly back from him to create the space I need to sign.

I shrug, signing that I'll accept whatever he thinks is right. He watches carefully, then nods at me, his expression warming, though only slightly. "Good answer. We'll make a decent sub out of you yet. Just possibly."

His eyes never leaving mine, he pulls a small, single key from his jeans pocket and hands it to me. I curl my fingers around it to make a fist, struck by the warmth of his body still remaining within the metal.

"This is the key to my dungeon. That's the door at the back, the one that was locked. I don't doubt you worked out what must be behind it."

It's a statement rather than a question, but I nod my agreement anyway.

"Go there. Let yourself in. I'd like you to undress, strip completely and leave your clothes on the floor outside the door. In the dungeon you'll see a mat on the floor, and there's a chain on the mat. The chain is for you to wear during your training here, with me. It goes around your waist. Do you understand its meaning?"

He pauses, one eyebrow raised as he awaits my response. I do understand the significance of accepting the chain. It signifies ownership, subservience, it's a pledge of obedience and acceptance, and it symbolizes the absolute authority of a Dom over his submissive. By agreeing to wear his chain around my waist, I am confirming my acceptance of those terms. I can take it off at any time, or he could take it from me, but whilst it's on, I'm his.

I nod my understanding and my acceptance. I'm clenching my fingers around the key, gripping so hard that my palm smarts under the pressure. His head inclines only slightly in acknowledgment, but in that moment our deal becomes real, the terms of our complex relationship crystallizing.

"Good. Once you're naked I want you to put the chain on, and then kneel on the mat and wait for me there. Do you understand?"

I nod once more, and he flicks his head toward the door to indicate I should get on with it. Now.

I turn, and leave the kitchen.

About the Author

Until 2010, Ashe was a director of a regeneration company before deciding there had to be more to life and leaving to pursue a lifetime goal of self-employment.

Ashe has been an avid reader of women's fiction for many years—erotic, historical, contemporary, fantasy, romance—you name it, as long as it's written by women, for women. Now, at last in control of her own time and working from her home in rural West Yorkshire, she has been able to realize her dream of writing erotic romance herself.

She draws on settings and anecdotes from her previous and current experience to lend color, detail and realism to her plots and characters, but her stories of love, challenge, resilience and compassion are the conjurings of her own imagination. She loves to craft strong, enigmatic men and bright, sassy women to give them a hard time—in every sense of the word.

When she's not writing, Ashe's time is divided between her role as resident taxi driver for her teenage daughter, and caring for a menagerie of dogs, cats, rabbits, tortoises and a hamster.

Ashe Barker loves to hear from readers. You can find her contact information, website details and author profile page at http://www.totallybound.com.

Totally Bound Publishing

Made in the USA
San Bernardino, CA
10 August 2017